THE
HELL RAISER

THE
HELL RAISER
by
RAY HOGAN

This first hardcover edition published in Great Britain 1990 by
SEVERN HOUSE PUBLISHERS LTD of
35 Manor Road, Wallington, Surrey SM6 0BW.
First published in hardcover format in the U.S.A. 1990 by
SEVERN HOUSE PUBLISHERS INC, New York.

British Library Cataloguing in Publication Data
Hogan, Ray
  The hell raiser.
  I. Title
  813.54 [F]

  ISBN 0–7278–4085–1

Distributed in the U.S.A. by
Mercedes Distribution Center, Inc.
62 Imlay Street, Brooklyn, New York 11231

Printed and bound in Great Britain by
Bookcraft (Bath) Ltd.

1

In the sudden, charged hush that dropped over the crowd in Wickenburg's Gold Bar saloon, Tom Zell pushed back slowly from his table. The two garishly dressed women sitting at either shoulder drew away hastily, giving him room as he faced the tall, thick-bodied miner glaring at him.

"Figured I'd catch you here with her," the big man said through clenched teeth. His hard, dark eyes were filled with a burning light and his bearded jaw was set to a square line.

Zell, a lean, wiry man in contrast to the miner's bulk, smiled indifferently. "Didn't know you were looking for me, Sackman."

"That's a damned lie," the miner shouted in a trembling voice. "I've been hunting Goldie since yesterday, and you know it! You had her and've been hiding out from me!"

Zell's features had colored slightly. "I—we've been right here," he said quietly, placing his hands on the table, palms down, fingers spread before him. "Anyway, what the hell business is it of yours?"

"Plenty," Sackman declared. "Goldie's my woman. You ain't got no right horning in, sweet-talking her away from me."

Tom Zell turned his head slightly, nodded at the

1

frowzy blonde who had been sitting to his left at the table but now was standing a few steps aside.

"That right, Goldie?"

The woman sniffed, brushed at her hair. "I ain't saying you did and I ain't saying you didn't. Point is, I ain't his woman. Never was, never will be."

A derby-hatted whiskey drummer at the bar laughed. "Way I heard it, Goldie's any man's woman—long as he's got a couple of dollars."

Sackman whirled, took a half-step toward the drummer. Immediately the bartender reached under his counter and produced a shotgun with shortened barrels.

"Never mind," he warned, shaking his head at the miner. "This here's gone about far enough. Do your quarreling outside. I don't aim to have my place busted up."

Sackman hesitated, mouth working convulsively, and then abruptly turned back to Zell. "Reckon I'll do my squaring up right here and now," he mumbled in a low voice.

"Best you back off, Henry," a man at a nearby table advised. "You'll get yourself killed. You ain't got a chance against Tom—and you know it."

"Maybe," Sackman replied.

"You saying you can stand up against him?"

"I got a scheme," the miner said confidently. "Figured it all out how I was going to square up with him when I heard he was here fooling around with Goldie."

The man at the table wagged his head. "Sack, you're looney. Best you turn around and walk out of here while you're still able."

"Nope, not yet," the miner said.

Tom Zell had not taken his gaze off the big miner.

"Listen to your friend," he said after a bit. "I don't want to kill you."

"That's just what you think you'll do, ain't it?" Sackman shouted. "You figure you're the best that ever come down the pike and there ain't nobody good as you when it comes to shooting—and that you can have any woman you take a fancy to!"

Zell, pale-blue eyes partly closed as anger now began to stir through him, shrugged. "Whatever you say," he murmured.

Leaning forward, he filled two of the three glasses on the table from the bottle he'd purchased earlier. Pushing one of the thick-bottomed containers at Sackman, he took up the other.

"Have a drink and we'll forget about this—both of us."

The miner's hand shot out. With a sweep of his arm, he knocked the glass to the floor.

"The hell with that! I ain't letting you weasel out of this!"

In the breathless quiet of the smoke-filled room Zell calmly downed his drink and set the empty glass back on the table. The crowd, sensing a sudden and violent climax to the confrontation, began to edge away.

"Knew this was coming," a voice somewhere along the bar declared. "Like Henry said, Zell seems to figure he's got a right to any woman he puts his eyes on."

"The woman's got something to do with it," a second voice pointed out. "Tom's maybe wilder'n hell and a good-time Charlie for sure, but they don't have to throw in with him. I ain't never heard of him twisting some gal's arm to get her into bed."

"Expect you're right, but he ought to use a bit of

sense about who he goes chasing after—another man's
woman, or maybe his wife—"

"You tell him that," a third man at the counter suggested with a short laugh. "I sure as the devil ain't
ever going to be the one."

Zell, his flat planed face emotionless, eyes narrowed
even more, considered Sackman coldly.

"Can see there's no talking you out of this—"

"Nope, there sure'n hell ain't," the miner replied.
"This here's one time you're getting what's coming to
you."

Somewhere in the saloon a bottle fell to the floor,
the crash followed immediately by the sound of cursing as a man vented his anger and frustration. But the
interruption did not decrease the tension. The moments ran on, taut, filled with guarded comments
from bystanders, and loaded with the promise of
death.

"It help any if I was to say Goldie's nothing to
me—only a friend?" Zell offered. "She's all yours far
as I'm concerned, and—"

"The hell I am!" the woman cut in before the
miner could reply. "I ain't nobody's!"

"You see what you've gone and done?" Sackman
demanded, pointing at her. "You've plain turned her
against me, fixed it so's she won't have nothing more
to do with me. I'm going to make you sorry you done
that, Zell!"

The bartender, shotgun in hand, had come from behind his counter. Moving hurriedly, he crossed to the
miner's side.

"Henry, I told you I wouldn't stand for no
ruckus," he warned sternly.

Sackman, fast for a man so large, spun. His big
hands wrapped about the twin barrels of the weapon,

and with a single jerk, wrenched it from the saloon-man's hands.

"You stay out of this, Ben," he yelled, and threw the gun into a far corner of the room.

The bartender, white-faced and shaken, fell back into the crowd and retreated toward the counter. Zell had come to his feet and, chair pushed back out of the way, was standing with shoulders sloped forward and hands hanging loosely at his sides.

"Let's get this over with," he said in a low voice. "I don't want it—none of it—and it's over nothing, but there's no making you see that."

"Nope, you ain't changing my mind," Sackman said, and then raising his voice so as to be heard throughout the saloon, added, "All right, boys!"

Two men, burly miners like Sackman, separated themselves from the crowd and moved up to stand beside him. Tom Zell considered them with no change of expression while Sackman's lips parted in a toothy smile.

"Brung along a little help," he said. "Knowed I couldn't take care of you by myself, so I got a couple of friends—Abe and Ollie Feek—to side me. I reckon that sort of evens things up."

2

John Nace paused at the edge of Wickenburg and surveyed the collection of shacks, false-fronted buildings, and cabins contemptuously. All frontier towns, it seemed to him, looked alike, the only difference being size.

He had by now become accustomed to what he termed their bleakness and accepted it as a product of a country where there always appeared to be plenty of everything but trees, grass, and water. Having lived his life so far along the broad, forever-flowing Ohio River, where such was taken for granted, the lack was not only conspicuous but appalling. He had been assured, however, that it would be different when he and the wagon train reached California.

Turning, Nace looked back to where the party had halted in the thin shade of several stunted trees. He could see Reuben Fisk, his squat, weather-hammered figure honed to strength by many years of labor in the fields, standing off to one side talking with Caleb Tolan, a man of similar build and like background. The latter's son, George, had, as was usual, paired off with Fisk's younger daughter, Purity. They were to be married once the train of three wagons reached their destination.

His wife, Abby, in conversation with the Fisks'

older daughter, Patience, was still sitting on the seat of their vehicle, her dissatisfaction with him apparent as always to the others. Abby's attitude could be mostly his fault, he supposed, as he'd always believed that a man should retain his position as the head of the house by showing firmness and resolve in all matters while his wife should tend strictly to womanly duties and ask no questions.

Fisk's wife, Martha, and Tolan's Lydia, although both much older than Abby—they being in their forties and she in her early twenties—appeared to be well-satisfied with that customary arrangement and it was hard to understand why Abby was not. But he had long since made up his mind to not fret about it. Abby would come around to his way of thinking eventually.

And his way—his stance of strong-minded, unyielding authority—was right. The proof of such was borne out by the fact that it was he the others had selected to lead the train west when it was decided to forsake their farms along the Ohio and move to a new land where they could live without fear of being flooded out annually; so far, they had no reason to regret their choice.

And now it was up to him to further demonstrate his ability by locating and hiring a reliable guide to conduct them safely through the Indian country that lay between Wickenburg and the Colorado River.

Moving on, Nace slanted for the first building that stood at the near end of the settlement's irregular street. A broad, patched, ramshackle affair, it bore a sign above its wide double doors that proclaimed it to be Haskell's Livery Barn. Entering the shadow-filled structure with its line of stalls down one side of a runway, Nace halted.

"Anybody here?" he called.

Immediately an elderly man in stained overalls, undershirt, and thick-soled shoes emerged from the darkness farther along and advanced to meet him.

"Sure is. I'm Pete Haskell. What's on your mind?"

Nace accepted the hand extended to him and shook it briefly. He gestured toward the wagons drawn up a short distance from the settlement.

"Name's John Nace. I'm heading that party of folks moving to California. Was told back a ways that there'd been Indian trouble west of here and that I'd best get myself a guide who could take us through."

"Apaches been giving us trouble all right," Haskell said, nodding. He had a florid complexion, dark eyes, gray beard and mustache, the tips of which he continually twisted and toyed with. "There was what some folks called a massacre near here last November."

"November—that's about four months ago. The Apaches still on the warpath?"

Haskell shrugged, brushed at the sweat on his forehead. "Ain't exactly what you'd call being on the warpath, but they're still hanging around, raiding some homesteader's or rancher's place now and then and jumping pilgrims moving across country."

"That's what I was told. Why ain't the army doing something about it?"

"I reckon they're doing what they can, but they're spread plenty thin. This here's big country and the army's mighty piddling for the job. Just ain't enough to go around, and anyways, it ain't just the Indians that's causing trouble. Got a lot of Mex *bandidos* and white trash—busters we call them—taking a hand in it."

"Busters? Why are they called that?"

"Jackleg miners—prospectors—come here on a shoestring expecting to hit it rich. Didn't, and then took to stealing and such to stay alive."

Nace gave that thought. It was not only the Indians they would have to guard against but Mexicans and white outlaws as well. So far they had encountered no such problems on the long trip from Ohio; now, when their journey was nearing its end, they were going to be confronted by danger from three different factions. That realization made the need for an experienced guide all the more pressing.

"Was told by the fellow who warned me about the Indians to hunt up a man named Zell and hire him to—"

"Tom Zell?" Haskell broke in. "That hell raiser?"

"That's the name," Nace replied. "It was said that nobody around here knew the country on west like him, and that he'd be the best man for the job."

Nace hesitated, the last words spoken by Haskell having their effect upon him. Thoughtful, he considered them, his eyes on a restless horse at the far end of the runway.

"Hell raiser," he echoed finally. "You mean he's a troublemaker?"

"Might say so," Haskell replied in a more restrained voice.

"What about him being a guide? It true what I was told about him being the best?"

"Yeh, reckon so—only he ain't no regular guide. Does hire out now and then to take folks here and there, same as he's done some cowboying and mining and riding shotgun for the stagecoaches and freight wagons—"

"Jack-of-all-trades," Nace commented scornfully.

"Guess that's right, too. Never has held a job for more'n a couple of months, same as he never in his life done anything good for somebody unless there was something in it for him. Main thing for him is women and whiskey—but I got to admit he's powerful good at what he does take a mind to do."

"You saying that even with all them drawbacks he—"

"Not saying they're drawbacks especially—just that he don't ever settle down to something for long."

"But despite all his drawbacks," Nace persisted, continuing where he was interrupted, "he'd be a good man to hire on as a guide?"

"Guide, gunfighter, wagonmaster—whatever you're wanting," the stableman agreed.

"You mentioned whiskey. He a heavy drinker?"

"Can say that for sure—but out here you can't fault a man for that. He's one of them kind, though, that it never seems to bother. Can't recollect ever seeing him stumbling drunk, same as I don't think I ever seen him when he wasn't drinking."

Nace again lost himself in consideration. Tom Zell appeared to be the man he needed, yet he had doubts as to the man's reliability. He supposed, however, he should see Zell, talk to him, and make up his own mind about that.

"Where'll I find him?"

Haskell's eyes opened in surprise. His thin shoulders stirred, and moving to the doorway, pointed down the near-deserted street to a two-storied structure standing at the intersection of a crossroad.

"There—at the Gold Bar Saloon—just a bit on past the Jail Tree," he said. "He hangs around there—and he'll either be upstairs in bed with some woman or he'll be downstairs drinking—and maybe fighting. . . . You still aim to hire him on?"

"Expect to talk to him," Nace said, stepping out into the afternoon's hot sunlight.

Haskell brushed nervously at his beard. "I'd just as soon you'd not say you was asking me about him—or tell him anything I said. Sure don't want no trouble with Tom Zell."

"I understand," Nace replied, smiling faintly, and moved off down the street.

There were few persons to be seen, one of whom was chained to a tree—the Jail Tree, Nace remembered Haskell had called it—but there appeared to be quite a number of the town's residents gathered at the Gold Bar Saloon.

Making his way through those standing in the street and on the landing, Nace reached the entrance and stepped inside. Something of interest was taking place, he reckoned, but he could see little from where he had stopped, and besides, he had no time for frivolities; it was important he find Zell and have a talk. Laying a hand on the arm of a man leaning against the inside door frame of the smoke-filled room, he smiled.

"Looking for a fellow named Tom Zell. Was told he'd likely be in here. Mind pointing him out to me?"

The man frowned, gave Nace a curious look, and then drawing the pilgrim a step farther into the saloon, leveled a finger at the opposite side of the wide room.

"That's him over there—about ready to do some killing."

3

A humorless smile pulled at Zell's lips as he studied the three men facing him from a dozen strides away. The crowd had fallen back completely now, leaving no one standing behind either Zell or Sackman and his friends.

"You're damn sure you want this?" Zell asked in a strong voice heard throughout the saloon.

"I'm here, ain't I?" the miner responded. "And you don't see me turning tail, do you?"

"Fact is," the shorter of the Feeks declared boldly, "we're aiming to do this here town a big favor and send you to the boneyard."

Zell shrugged. "Could be, but don't take no bets on it."

The whiskey drummer, caught up in the hush and tension that hung like a stifling cloud inside the saloon, coughed nervously and spat into the nearest cuspidor.

"Those odds—three to one—that's mighty bad," he said in a low voice. "I don't see how that fellow Zell, good as you claim he is, stands a chance against—"

"I'd say the odds are about right," the man next to him observed dryly. "He's lightning fast with that gun he carries, and Sackman and his friends would be better off with pick handles."

12

"Was it a free-for-all I'd sort of lean toward them," someone else commented.

"Not me! I wouldn't bet against Tom Zell even then," another bystander said.

Zell, if he was conscious of the hoarsely whispered words, gave no sign. To him they were only small, remote sounds intentionally kept at a distance that he might better concentrate on the business at hand.

A tall, muscular man in his mid-twenties, he had a shock of thick dark hair that contrasted sharply with pale-blue, almost-gray eyes. His face was angular, with a high, wide forehead, a straight nose, and a somewhat large mouth. The mustache, trimmed to fit his upper lip, was full, and at that moment a thick stubble of dark beard was on his cheeks and chin.

The boots he wore were from cattle country, as were the cord pants, the blue shield shirt, the leather vest, and the bandanna. But the hat—flat-crowned and not too wide of brim—was more of the plainsman type.

"Anytime," he called softly to the miners.

All were well-armed, Sackman carrying a pistol in his belt, the Feeks each with a holstered gun on their hips. Zell, his steady gaze on them, took all such into consideration.

He had no idea how good any of the three was with a weapon. Miners, as a rule, were far more adept with clubs and fists, but Tom had long ago made it a hard-and-fast rule to never take anything for granted. Any man who called him out was dangerous until proven otherwise.

"I'm asking you again—do your fighting outside," the saloon owner said in a plaintive voice.

Sackman shook his head. "I ain't moving. This is going to get finished right here and—now!"

Zell reacted instantly when he saw the break in the miner's expression and heard the word that apparently was the prearranged signal. His hand whipped down, came up fast as he lunged to one side. The room rocked with the explosion of his pistol. As the echoes sprang to life and began to bounce back and forth within the four walls of the saloon and powder smoke bulged upward to mingle with that of cigars, pipes, and cigarettes hovering near the ceiling, he triggered his weapon a second time—and then a third.

Henry Sackman was going down even before he could bring his gun into play. The taller of the Feek brothers, if that was their relationship, managed to get off one shot before Zell's second bullet smashed into his chest and drove life from his body. The other fared little better, firing his pistol once, missing cleanly, and then staggering back and falling to the floor when Tom Zell's third bullet drilled into him with its shocking force.

A stillness hung over the breathless crowd gathered in the Gold Bar Saloon as the acrid smell of gunpowder spread throughout its length and breadth, and then as if suddenly aware that it was all over, the twin lines of bystanders broke and surged toward the fallen men.

"This'n—Sackman—is dead," a man bending over the miner announced.

"So's Abe," another voice added. "Ollie's still breathing—barely. Somebody better go get Doc Winters."

Zell, unmoving, raised his pistol and slowly, methodically, punched the empty brass casings from its cylinder. That done, he thumbed fresh cartridges from the loops of the belt he wore, and reloaded.

"Somebody ought to get the undertaker, too—"

"I'm here." The response came from deep in the crowd. "If you gentlemen will just step aside, give me and my boy room—"

Tom Zell turned away at that point, settled back down to his table. There was no sign of either of the two women, he noted as he poured himself a drink, and that brought a wry smile to his lips.

"Was the fastest dang thing I've ever seen," a man said, coming to a halt before him.

Zell made no reply, merely nodded, and the fellow faded back into the milling crowd. At that moment the whiskey drummer, still at the bar, caught his attention, and raising his glass in a congratulatory salute, downed his liquor in a quick gulp.

"Was not a fair fight—I got to say it—"

Tom swung his attention about, faced the speaker, a squat, round-eyed man in a dusty blue suit. Hannemeyer—one of the mine bosses.

"So?" Zell drawled, shrugging.

"You knew damn well they didn't stand a chance against you!"

"Tried telling Sackman that. So'd a couple of his friends. He wouldn't listen."

"You could have walked away, refused to shoot it out with them."

Zell shook his head. Refilling his glass, he glanced around the room. Volunteers were picking up the bodies of Sackman and Abe Feek, assisting the undertaker in removing them. Ollie still lay where he had fallen, the doctor not yet having put in an apearance.

"No," Zell said, "I don't walk away. Never have and never will. Sackman and his sidekicks wanted it, and when I couldn't change their minds, I had to go through with it."

"He's right," a man standing nearby said. "There

just wasn't nothing else he could do. Just didn't have no choice."

"Killing ain't never the answer," Hannemeyer declared stubbornly, "and I aim to take this up with the marshal when he gets back. And if he won't do nothing about it, I'll call up a miner's court, see if I can get some justice. We're supposed to be civilized around here and not like them murdering savages and cutthroats running loose—"

"Town ain't likely to get civilized, as you say, as long as we've got them Apaches and Mex and renegades to deal with, and you know it. And if it wasn't for men like Zell—"

Tom listened idly to the exchange. It was nothing new; he'd heard it all before, and several times had been the cause of the discussion just as he was this fine day in an unusually warm March.

"Well, have it your way," the mine boss said, wiping at the sweat on his anger-flushed cheeks, "but I'm promising you people ain't heard the last of this. It ain't only the law I'm talking about, but Henry Sackman has plenty of friends—and so's the Feeks. Won't surprise me none if they don't gang up and come looking to square things up with you, Zell."

Tom played with his empty glass, twirling it between thumb and forefinger on the table. The saloon was still crowded; more curious onlookers, having gotten word of the excitement, came to have their look and ask their questions, thus increasing the hubbub. Winters, the town physician, had finally arrived and was now bending over Ollie Feek making his examination. As Zell watched, the doctor straightened up and shook his head in the time-honored way of medical men expressing hopelessness.

"You hear me?"

At the question Zell refilled his empty glass. "Yeh," he murmured, downing the liquor, "and I've heard it all before. Let 'em come."

4

As the guns crashed, loading the saloon with a thunderous roar and pungent, billowing smoke, John Nace stood transfixed.

He was horrified, awed by the swift violence, the sudden, irrevocable occurrence of death. He had seen men die before accidentally or from natural causes, but never had he stood by and witnessed a shoot-out—a deliberate contest in which the faster man survived.

"God! Ain't that Zell something?" the man near the wall muttered admiringly. "There ain't nobody—no, sir, nobody—that can outdraw and outshoot him!"

Nace nodded woodenly. The Gold Bar Saloon now was noisy with excited voices, and through the confusion he heard someone advise all present that somebody named Sackman was dead while another voice stated that Abe had encountered a similar fate. Ollie, a third man, was barely alive and the doctor should be called.

Rigid, still in the throes of shock, John Nace stared out across the turbulent room. Tall, almost cadaverous, he was a serious, intent individual with thick, dark hair, small, black eyes, and a firm set jaw. He wore a full mustache but otherwise was clean-shaven—a duty he performed religiously upon rising each morning regardless of circumstance or conditions.

A farmer by legacy, he hoped to pyramid the profits from such—which he'd found impossible to do in Ohio, thanks to the vagaries of nature—into a mercantile business once he and his wife were settled in the new land and had matters under control.

Zell, he noted at that moment, was calmly reloading his pistol. The man had just killed two human beings—possibly three—yet he was standing there in the drifting smoke accepting plaudits from close-by admirers as indifferently as if he'd just won a spelling bee!

A tremor shook Nace. Tom Zell was a killer—a heartless, cold-blooded murderer—and Nace wasn't sure he wanted to have anything to do with him. Pivoting, he started for the door. The man he'd spoken to earlier looked about in surprise.

"Ain't you going to see Zell?"

"Later—maybe," Nace replied, and stepping out onto the saloon's landing, entered the street.

Cutting left, he headed back up the dusty lane, his mind working on the problem he now faced: his failure to hire Tom Zell, and why. He was not certain of just how Fisk and Tolan would react; they took a different view from him on many things, and there were times when the disturbing thought came to him that he'd been chosen leader of the wagon train not for his wisdom but because of his younger years. It had been more or less agreed that Zell, recommended to them as the best, should be . . .

"What was that there shooting all about?"

At the question John Nace drew to a stop. He had drawn abreast the livery stable, and unaware of it, had all but walked past its owner, Pete Haskell.

"A killing—two, maybe three men. Were miners, I heard it said."

"Was it Zell that done it?"

"It was," Nace replied grimly. "Stood there just looking at them. Then there was shooting and all three of the miners went down."

"Way it works when Tom Zell's taking a hand in it," Haskell said. "You hear who the miners were?"

"One was named Sackman. Another—"

"Sackman," the stable owner cut in. "I recollect hearing somebody say there was bad feelings between them over one of the girls at the saloon."

"Wouldn't know about that," Nace continued. "Two others were called Abe and Ollie. Never caught the last names."

"They'd be the Feeks—brothers. Seen them running with Sackman. Worked the same mine."

"One called Ollie wasn't dead, but they didn't figure he'd live. It was a terrible thing."

Haskell pushed his hat to the back of his head, clawed at his beard. "Why're you saying that? Was something that had to be settled."

"But for this Zell to shoot down—kill—"

"Sounds to me like the odds were all with Henry Sackman and the Feeks. They had guns, didn't they?"

"Yes, but Zell's an expert with a pistol while those miners probably weren't much."

"Except it was them that pushed it—and you can bet they all three knowed how good Zell is with a gun. I reckon there ain't nobody around who don't." Haskell paused, looked more closely at Nace. "You look to me like you'd been about the right age for the war; you seen killing there—ain't no difference here in this. Killing's killing and dead's dead no matter how it comes about."

Nace remained silent, glanced toward the wagons. Fisk and Tolan were making an adjustment of some sort in the harness of the latter's team.

"I was in the war, all right," he said finally. "Never saw any action. Was at a desk for the two years I served handling claims."

"I see," Haskell murmured. Then, "I take it you never talked to Tom about hiring him."

"No."

"Still aim to?"

"No, I don't think so. I don't hold with murder."

"You can't say it was murder—not if Sackman and the Feeks had guns and was figuring to shoot Zell. Now, I ain't no big friend of Tom Zell's, but the man sure as the devil had a right to stand up—to defend himself. That's the way it is out here—a fellow sure better look out for hisself because there ain't nobody else going to—"

"The law's supposed—"

"Law? Friend, you're going to find it sure ain't like it was where you come from! First off, lawmen are few and far between, and second, most of the time they won't be anxious to step in and collar a man like Tom Zell—too risky. And third, you're going to find out that sometimes the law ain't no better'n the outlaw."

Nace rubbed at his smooth jaw. He had been aware of such ever since they'd crossed the Missouri, but it had never really registered fully on his mind. Accustomed to an orderly, routine way of life in association with law-abiding citizens, he had simply taken for granted that the new West, though somewhat unsettled, was actually little different from what it was along the Ohio.

"What're you aiming to do if you don't hire on Zell?" Haskell asked.

Both he and Nace had turned, were now looking down the street to the front of the Gold Bar Saloon. Several men had come out into the open and were conversing in small groups.

"Wanted to asked you if there was another man I could get."

The stable owner again scratched at his beard. "Just can't think of nobody right at this minute," he said doubtfully. "And whoever, he sure won't be as good for what you're wanting as Zell. He knows the shortcuts he can take where the Mex and the Apaches ain't likely to be hanging about. Was it me looking for what you need, I'd hire him on—was he willing."

Nace frowned. "Willing? You think he might not be?"

"Ain't nobody knows for sure what Zell would do, 'cepting Zell hisself. Never has been one to do no more work than he just has to. He'd rather spend his time with a woman and a bottle of whiskey. Reckon you could say that's what tops the pile for him— women and whiskey and then maybe eating. After them'll come working."

Nace stirred, gaze still on the groups in front of the Gold Bar Saloon. The number had increased, and he wondered what was taking place that was of such interest. Did it have something to do with the killings— with Tom Zell?

"You mind scratching your memory and seeing if you can think of another good man you'd recommend to me?" he said then, after a time. "I don't like the idea of heading out for the Colorado River without somebody that knows the way."

"That ain't no problem," Haskell replied. "If a

man'll just pull out, head west, he'll come to the Colorado. And then if he crosses over and keeps on going due west, he'll end up at the ocean—and California. It's what he's liable to run into between here and there that'll put him in a peck of trouble."

"I understand—"

"Way I see it, you're making a hell of a big mistake letting your feelings about that shoot-out keep you from hiring him. Something like that happens pretty regular out here in this part of the country. It's just the way things gets settled sometimes—the only way, in fact. But if you want me to try and scare up somebody else that'll take you across the desert, I'll sure do it."

"I'll be mighty obliged," Nace said, and moved off toward the wagons. "Can look for me to drop by about dark."

5

"You get him?" Caleb Tolan asked as Nace drew near.

John shook his head. "Nope—and I'm not sure I want him."

Fisk turned away from whatever he was doing with a trace chain, frowned. Waiting until Nace had come to a halt, he wiped his thick-fingered hands on a bit of rag, spat a stream of brown tobacco juice at a nearby rock, and squinted.

"Now, what in tarnation does that mean?"

There was no missing the note of impatience in the older man's tone. Nace looked beyond him and Tolan. The women, aware of his return, were coming out from behind the wagons where they had been resting in the shade of the arching tops. All were staring at him wonderingly, having heard his answer to Tolan's question.

"Man's just not the kind we want around," Nace said, and repeated all he could remember of Pete Haskell's words, finishing up with: "He's a killer."

"Killer? How do you know that?" Tolan demanded.

"Saw it with my own eyes. I watched him shoot down three men—murder them in cold blood."

24

Fisk said, "Heard what sounded like gunshots. Reckon that was it. What was it all about?"

"Over some painted woman, near as I could tell. Seems to be the kind he is—a drinker and a woman-chaser. This fellow I talked to—Haskell—said he was a bad one."

"What'd he say about him being a guide?"

Nace shrugged, eyes on his wife. Abby had turned about and was walking slowly back to their wagon.

"Claimed he was the best around, that he didn't know anybody as good."

"He have somebody else in mind that we could hire?" Fisk wanted to know, his tone still sharp.

"Promised to do some thinking, try to come up with a name. Told him I'd come back later."

"But he figures he won't have much luck," Tolan said heavily. "What'd he think about us going on without a guide?"

"Well, there's been plenty of trouble, not only with the Indians—Apaches—but with Mexican and American outlaws, too. I gathered it wasn't safe to try crossing the desert unless you've got plenty of company."

"Then, way I see it, we best go right ahead and hire this fellow Zell," Fisk said."

Nace shrugged. "If he'll hire out."

The older man frowned, leveled an irritated glance at John Nace. "Seems you didn't find out much of anything while you was down there. Ain't he for hire?"

"Depends on how he happens to be feeling. Like I've told you, he's mainly interested in women and whiskey."

"But you ain't talked to him, so you don't know, do you?" Fisk said, and swiped at his face with a faded bandanna. The day was warm and a man doing only a small amount of labor quickly raised a sweat.

"No. Saloon was crowded and there was a lot of people moving about and talking and telling him what a great fellow he was."

"Reckon he's all that for certain," Tolan observed. "Any man who can stand and shoot it out with three others—and come out alive—has got to be something!"

"Sounds to me like he's just the one we need," Martha Fisk said, agreeing. She was a short stocky woman with a gray, washed-out look to her.

Nace considered her gravely. "Now, Martha, do you want a man like this Zell around your daughters?"

"Maybe we don't have a choice," Lydia Tolan pointed out. Unlike Martha, she was thin to emaciation, but what she lacked in physical structure she made up in will and stubbornness. "I think we ought to hire the devil himself if that's what it'll take to get us to California."

Abby Nace had come forward again and was listening to what was being said. Ordinarily she took no hand in dicussions and decisions of this sort, simply left it up to her husband to speak for both of them, but in this particular instance she apparently wanted to be heard.

"I don't think we ought to let the man's reputation bother us, either," she said. "I want to get to California—and I want to get there alive. If this Zell is what we'll have to have, then I vote we hire him."

Nace favored his wife with a rebuking glance. "You don't know what you're saying, Abby. I—"

"Maybe she does," Tolan cut in. "If we'll be risking our necks without him then let's get him."

"Could stay here—wait for another wagon train," Nace suggested.

"Now, you know we can't do that," Tolan stated flatly. "It's already took us longer'n we figured it would."

Nace stirred indifferently. He had hoped his decision to not hire Tom Zell would go unchallenged, but the exact opposite had occurred—even where his own wife was concerned. But he reckoned he could understand her attitude; she was sick of being on the road, of riding in a wagon, of seeing nothing but empty desolation day after day.

If the truth were known, he guessed that Abby was not alone, that all the others felt the same. As for himself, he certainly could not get to California any too soon; the quicker he got there and put the land to work, the sooner his plan to build a general mercantile store would get underway.

"Don't mean to go again' you, John," Tolan said, "but I reckon we all better have a say in this."

George Tolan, just turned nineteen, a quiet, intent, blond man looking forward to a life with Purity Fisk, nodded to his father. "Could take a vote."

"What I'm meaning," the older Tolan said. "Everybody."

"Women, too," Lydia added firmly.

The men exchanged glances. Nace started to make a comment, but Reuben Fisk spoke first.

"Yeh, I expect they're entitled to a say in something like this, seeing as how their necks'll be on the block, same as ours."

Nace brushed at his jaw. This wasn't the way he believed it should be handled. Matters of such importance rightfully should be left to the men of the families. Women, he felt, were too inclined to listen to their hearts and thus make foolish decisions that could have dire results. But if that was what they all wanted . . .

"Hardly think we need to vote," he said. "You've all spoken your mind, and it's plain to me that you think we ought to hire Zell."

"Well, don't you?" Tolan pressed.

Nace's shoulders lifted, fell. "Can't say that I—"

"Somebody's coming," George Tolan announced abruptly.

With the others, Nace came about and faced into the direction of the settlement. A man riding a bay was approaching. He sat erect in the saddle, rode with the easy grace of one at home on a horse.

Reuben Fisk stepped up beside Nace, and taking the customary precaution motioned to George, directing him to get a weapon.

Nace shook his head as recognition of the oncoming rider came to him. "It's all right."

The horseman drew to a halt before them. Removing the plainsman's hat he was wearing, he nodded to the women, who stood a bit apart from the men.

"Ladies," he said, bowing slightly to them, and then shifted his attention to Nace and the others. "Name's Tom Zell. Was told one of you came to town looking for me. I'm here asking why."

6

Zell, slack in his saddle, right hand resting carelessly
on the butt of the pistol holstered at his side, waited
for an answer. Three wagons of pilgrims—homesteaders, he saw; four men, about the same number of
women, three of which aroused his interest. One—tall,
well-shaped, with dark hair and brows and clear blue
eyes—was studying him intently, a faint smile on her
nicely curved lips. The others—blondes with brown
eyes, young and undoubtedly sisters—were also giving
him thorough consideration.

He responded to all three with a second polite in-
clination of his head and settled his attention on the
men, one of whom had moved forward a step.

"Was me. The name's John Nace," the pilgrim said.
"Was told to look you up."

"Why?"

"Step down and we'll talk about it," one of the
older men, remembering his manners, invited. "I'm
Reuben Fisk—since John there sort of forgot to do
any introducing. Woman in the checkered apron's my
wife, Martha."

"And I'm Caleb Tolan," Zell heard the other older
man state as he accepted the offer to dismount. "Lady
next to Martha's my wife, Lydia—and that young fellow there's our son, George."

29

Tom gravely shook hands all around and then paused before the one person in the party he was the most interested in meeting—the willowy brunette.

"My wife, Abby," Nace said hurriedly.

Zell smiled, nodded, encouraged by the welcome in the woman's eyes, and then turned to the two girls waiting beside Reuben Fisk. He paused expectantly. Immediately the sodbuster filled the break.

"These are my daughters, Mr. Zell. Tall one's Patience. Other one is Purity."

Again Zell acknowledged the introduction with a polite nod. "A man ought to be right proud to have a pair of beautiful daughters like you and your missus have," Tom said. Patience, a bit on the lean side, would be about nineteen, he guessed. Purity, who was smiling broadly and filled out the dress she was wearing to perfection, was likely no more than seventeen.

"I—we are," Fisk said. "Martha and me sure are. Purity's engaged. She's going to marry young Tolan when we get to California."

"That's why I was looking for you," Nace said, apparently a bit impatient with all the side talk.

Zell flicked a final glance at the woman, Abby, and placed his cool attention on Nace, evidently the wagonmaster of the train—if the leader of one so small was entitled to the term.

"Was there—in the Gold Bar Saloon—all day."

Nace shrugged. "Well, you were a bit—I guess I could say busy when I got there. Figured it was best not to bother you."

A faint smile cracked Zell's mouth. "I savvy. You walked in on the shooting. It was over and done with in a few minutes. Should've hung around a bit. I would've bought you a drink and we could talk over whatever it is you've got on your mind. Fellow you talked to there said you didn't mention what it was."

"Haskell—the livery stableman? He knew—"

"Not him. Was a jasper that hangs around the saloon—don't know his name. Said you asked for me then took off right after the shooting and headed for here. . . . What's it all about?"

"We're needing a guide—somebody to take us across the desert, get us safely to the Colorado River. We're headed for California."

"Was a fellow back up a ways that recommended you to us," Fisk added when Nace made no mention of the fact.

Zell, hat tipped forward on his head, brushed at his mustache thoughtfully. "Recall his name?"

"No," Nace replied, taking charge again. "Was a storekeeper and the town was called Bitter Springs, I think."

Tom Zell nodded. "Would be Dave Santee. Runs a saloon, however, not a general store."

Nace's features tightened slightly. Fisk and Tolan exchanged smiles.

"That's him," the latter said. "We'd heard there was trouble between here and the Colorado, and asked him about it when we was having a drink. Told us we'd heard right, that it'd be plenty risky trying to get through, especially since we was such a small party, and that we'd best line us up a guide. Mentioned something about a massacre."

"Was last November," Zell said, drawing a leather cigar case from his shirt pocket. Selecting one of the slim, black stogies for himself, after offering them around and finding no takers, he thumbnailed a match into a tiny flame and lit the weed.

"Folks call it the Wickenburg Massacre," he said,

blowing a cloud of smoke into the motionless hot air. "Was a stagecoach. It was carrying seven people—one of them a woman named Mollie Shepard. It was said she was carrying about fifteen thousand dollars' worth of jewelry and cash in her baggage. And there was another fifty thousand that an army man named Kruger—the quartermaster—had with him.

"Stage was jumped west of here about seven miles and everybody was killed except Mollie and Kruger. They managed to duck into the brush, although they'd both been hit. When the mail coach came across them a time later, they were in pretty bad shape, and by the time they got here Kruger was about dead."

"Was it Indians—Apaches?" Tolan asked.

"Some doubt. Mollie said they were all wearing long army coats—there were nine of them—and she couldn't tell for sure. Kruger claimed they were Indians and had no doubt about it in his mind. The tracks found around the coach—all moccasin—sort of bore out his claim and convinced a lot of people."

"You sound like you had some doubts," Fisk commented.

Zell shrugged. "Got my own opinion. Will say this, the only baggage that was opened was Mollie's and the quartermaster's, so whoever it was knew what they were looking for. Mollie had a lot of fancy-colored clothes—the kind that would sure take an Indian's eye—but they weren't touched, were just left there. And the horses weren't driven off, either, which sure doesn't sound like Apaches."

"Then it was outlaws—"

"That's the way I see it," Zell said, agreeing. "Was either Mexicans or Americans—or both. Could've been some Indians mixed up in it, but I don't think so."

"That was about four months ago," Nace said. "You think the same bunch is still hanging around?"

"Who knows? There's been trouble right along, so it could be them, or another gang. I can think of three parties that got hit and turned around and came back. They claimed they'd been jumped by Indians and Mex riding together and were robbed of everything they had that was worth anything. And there was one case where a young girl about the age of your youngest there, Fisk, was carried off. Heard not long ago that the menfolk in her family were still hunting her."

Martha Fisk gasped. "You mean they kidnapped her?"

"Yes, ma'am, that's what I mean," Zell said, and broke off any further explanation detailing the victim's undoubted fate.

Caleb Tolan shook his head. "That's a mighty sad thing. . . . How long will it take us to reach the Colorado?"

Zell glanced at the wagons, at the teams and extra horses. "Four days—more or less. Could be a bit longer, depending."

"That long?" Lydia Tolan said in a falling voice. "We'd hoped—"

"And it'd be risky now, the way things stand," Zell continued. "You'd be smart to hold off until later on. Maybe the army'll bring in some more troopers—or there could be another wagon train come through and you could throw in with them. That'd be my recommendation."

"We can't wait," Reuben Fisk said flatly. "We've got to keep moving no matter what."

7

Zell pulled off his flat-crowned hat, brushed at his thick, dark hair. "What's the big hurry?" he asked, replacing the headgear to a greater angle as he sought to shade his eyes from the sun.

"People're holding land for us up there in California," Fisk explained. "About five hundred acres we aim to split up and work—farm. Sent a deposit to bind the deal, but there's a time limit."

"And the time's about up," Caleb Tolan added. "If we don't make it by the deadline, we won't only lose the binder, but we'll lose out on the land, too."

"There's land in Oregon to be had," Zell said, watching Abby Nace walk languidly to one of the wagons and disappear behind it. "Or you could turn around, go back to where you came from. No disgrace in that. Plenty of folks have done that when they found out this country wasn't all it had been cracked up to be."

"Nothing to go back to," John Nace said. "We're farmers, and the places we had along the Ohio River are gone—"

"Got washed out just about every year," Fisk said. "Things'd be going along real good and it'd look like we were due to come out on top. Then the river would catch us and we'd maybe lose everything but

34

what we had on our backs and could tote to high ground. Man gets mighty tired of that—working like a dog eighteen hours a day for months and then losing it all in a couple of hours."

"Tough all right," Tom said. Abby, he noted, had pulled a lace shawl about her shoulders, had also taken a few moments to fluff and pin back her hair.

"We got a chance to sell out, all of us, to an outfit that wanted to build a dock and set up some kind of a shipping company," Nace continued. "We took their offer, got lined up for the land in California through a broker, and headed out, but traveling went slower than we figured and we got behind. Like Reuben said, we're up against a deadline."

Zell nodded his understanding. The party faced a big problem, that was certain. Inexperienced and too few in number to defend themselves against outlaws or Indians, they likely would never make it alive to the Harcuvar Mountains—and with several young women in the train, God help them if the renegades happened to be comancheros!

"Still think you'd be smart to hold off, wait for another wagon train if you're set against turning back."

"Told why we can't do that," Fisk said heavily. "Got to keep going. We've done burned all our bridges behind us."

"We hoped we could hire you to take us through," Nace said tentatively.

Zell brushed at his mouth. "No, don't think I'm interested. Wrong time."

"Hate to hear that. Can you give us the name of another man—one that we could depend on?"

Tom gave that thought. His gaze was on Abby once again, now standing with the other women. She was a hell of a good-looker, the kind that could sure turn a man inside out when she took the notion.

"No, sure can't, at least nobody you'd want to stake your lives on," he said, answering Nace's question.

Fisk sighed heavily and turned away. The man's wife quickly laid a hand on his slumped shoulders

"Don't give up, Reuben," Zell heard her say. "We've got this far, we'll find a way to go on."

"How? We can't risk everything—the girls—"

"Maybe we could go into town and hire men as outriders," Nace suggested. "Could line up a dozen or so, and even if it cost us a lot, it'd be worth it."

And just about as chancy as heading out with no protection at all, Zell told himself. Even if a dozen such riders could be recruited, there'd be no guarantee they'd not turn on the Ohio party and strip them of everything they had.

What the hell, he supposed he could take on the job, although it was one that a man sure couldn't be too keen about. The risk of being jumped would be high—much higher than usual, since a train of three wagons was so small—but, he realized, his eyes on Abby, who was still watching him with that small, provocative smile on her lips, he'd taken risks before and managed to come through.

Further, he was not forgetting what that mine boss, Hannemeyer, had said—not that he feared reprisal from the friends of Henry Sackman and the Feeks; he could handle that with no trouble. But he was already at odds with Wickenburg's marshal over another shooting, and when the lawman learned of the Sackman affair, well, the lid would really blow off the kettle! And if he should happen to have it out with Sackman's miner friends and a couple of them ended up dead, then matters would go sky-high and the old marshal would undoubtedly order him to leave town and stay out—something he wasn't ready to do.

"Are you sure you won't reconsider, Mr. Zell?"

Tom glanced up. It was Abby. She had come forward and was standing before him. Her eyes were slightly almond-shaped, he noted, and her skin had the healthy color of rich cream. Her voice was level, a bit on the low side, which probably meant she could sing up a storm if she desired.

"Been mulling it about in my head," Zell said, reveling in the good, clean smell of her—one devoid of cheap perfume and face powder. "Just happens I'm not doing anything special right now, and I sure wouldn't sleep nights if I let you folks head out on your own."

Fisk had spun around. "You mean you'll take the job?" he fairly shouted.

Tom nodded, but he was hearing the homesteader as if from a distance. Abby Nace's smile was claiming his attention.

"When do you want to move out?" he asked then after the flurry of comments had subsided.

"In the morning," Tolan said promptly.

"That jake with you?" Fisk asked. "Now, if you've got business to tend to first, we can hold off for another day."

The stogie, held alternately between fingers and teeth had long since gone out, and raising his hand, Zell flipped the weed a distance.

"Was thinking of you," he said. "Thought you might want to rest yourselves and your stock, and maybe do some repair work on your wagons."

"We're all in good shape—same with the livestock and the wagons," Fisk said. "Ain't no need hanging around on our part."

"Can't see any reason why we can't move out in the morning at first light."

"Fine! Fine!" Tolan said, rubbing his hands together. Lydia, his wife, had wheeled and gathered Martha Fisk in her arms.

"I knew our prayers would be answered," she declared, tears sparkling in her eyes.

"Hold on a minute," Nace called, bringing them all to attention. "We best find out what this is going to cost, see if we can afford it."

"We've got to afford it, John," Fisk said, "otherwise we stand to lose everything. But I expect Mr. Zell's a reasonable man."

"Like to think so," Zell said. "One thing, right here at the start, I'd like for you all to call me Tom. That mister I've been hearing makes me uncomfortable, like I was wearing a stiff collar and a black tie."

"You got a price in your head?" Nace pressed, unwilling to let the question of cost die. "We all know it's going to be a dangerous journey and—"

"How does a hundred dollars suit you?" Zell cut in.

Nace bobbed. Caleb Tolan said, "Sounds real good—reasonable. I'll admit I was expecting us to have to pay more, considering the risk."

"I aim to try and dodge the risks," Zell said. "Now, if you're agreeable, I'll get my gear and stay the night with you so's we can get an early start in the morning. I'd as soon the town didn't know when we pulled out and what trail we took."

"You're plenty welcome," Fisk said. "Just pick yourself a spot."

"And don't bother about food," Abby said. "You can eat with us—John and me—"

Zell smiled, nodded. "I'm obliged—"

"We'll all share with you, Tom," Tolan said. "You

can take turns, have your meals first with one of us and then the other."

"Sounds good," Zell said, glancing at Abby. And then, touching the brim of his hat with a forefinger, he turned on a heel, smiled at the others, and crossed to his horse.

"I'll see you all later," he said, and swinging up into the saddle, rode off toward town.

8

Shortly before sundown Tom Zell returned to the camp, bringing with him his rifle, extra ammunition, blanket roll, and saddlebags containing other personal items he felt would be necessary. He would not be away from Wickenburg for long, he'd realized—ten days at the most—thus was traveling fairly light.

Greeted with smiles of welcome, he rode to the edge of the camp, and halting, dropped his gear in a level place screened by brush a dozen yards or so from the nearest wagon, which happened to be the Naces'.

Supper was ready not long after his arrival, and accepting the invitation extended him earlier by Abby Nace, he crossed to their fire and at John Nace's direction seated himself at their small, improvised table. He was feeling relaxed and at ease, having treated himself to a drink of whiskey from the bottle in his saddlebags.

"I'm sure obliged to you folks," he said as Abby set plates heaped with fried potatoes, beans cooked with chunks of ham, greens, and hot biscuits before him and her husband. "Not often a man like me gets to enjoy this kind of a meal."

Nace only nodded and began to eat at once. Zell, waiting for Abby to sit down to her plate, glanced about at the other members of the train. All, with the exception of the Fisk girls, were busy at their suppers. Purity and Patience had turned, were watching him with close interest. Tom nodded and smiled in response, and then as Abby came to take her place at the table, he rose slightly and put his attention on her.

John Nace said, "I'm curious about one thing, Zell."

Tom pushed his cup toward Abby that she might more easily fill it with coffee—or chicory, he wasn't sure which. "About what?"

"That shooting. Two, or I expect I ought to say three, men died. Anywhere else the law would have put you behind bars, where you would have remained until you could stand trial for murder. Here—"

"Here a man has to be his own law," Tom cut in curtly. He would as soon not speak of the incident—especially in front of Abby—but she had paused and appeared to be awaiting eagerly his reply. "He has to be. Would have been different if it hadn't been a fair fight—say, they didn't have guns and weren't trying to kill me. Then the crowd would have stepped in and I would have found myself chained to the Jail Tree while they got a miner's court together."

"But there was killing. Seems to me the law—"

"You'll find it's not like it was back in Ohio," Zell said, and smiled at Abby. "This meal is delicious, Mrs. Nace. I can't recall ever enjoying food more."

The woman flushed with pleasure. "Thank you—and please call me Abby. Now, there's pie—dried apple—when you're ready."

"At your convenience," Zell said, refilling his cup.

It was pleasant there in the camp, made cheerful by the laughing and talking of the members, the bright fires, and the warm, still air heavy with the odor of mesquite and fairyduster blossoms. Tom was glad he had agreed to conduct the train across the desert to the Colorado. Besides the promising prospects afforded by the presence of Abby Nace and the Fisk sisters—particularly the younger one, Purity—it would be a change and an enjoyment just to be around their kind for a spell.

Abruptly John Nace got to his feet. Abby, approaching with generous proportions of the pie she'd mentioned, frowned, paused.

"Need to talk some things over with Caleb and Reuben," he said, and pivoting, walked quickly to where the two older men were settling down with their pipes.

Abby shrugged, resumed her place at the table. Setting Zell's plate of dessert before him, she smiled apologetically. "John will eat his piece later," she murmured.

Tom made no comment, but Nace's cold treatment of his wife, the continual ignoring and inattention, had not escaped his attention. Finishing the pastry, he settled back.

"More?" Abby asked quickly.

Zell shook his head, grinned. "Best I say no. A man could founder on the kind of meals you put out, Abby."

Color again mounted in the woman's cheeks. "I'm glad you enjoyed it."

Zell reached into a pocket for his cigar case. Selecting one of the stogies, he held it up for her to see. "Tobacco annoy you?"

"Not at all," she replied. "In fact, I enjoy the smell. John doesn't smoke—Pa, my father, did. I used to miss it, but I've gotten used to that, just like I've grown used to many things."

There was a wistful note in Abby Nace's voice apparent to Zell as he struck a match and held it to the tip of his stogie. Earlier he had suspected that the woman was far from happy, and now was convinced. He wondered what the reason might be.

"Everything changes," he said.

"Yes, I suppose so. Have you always lived here in this part of the country?"

"Born in Texas. Folks had a place there—on the Brazos River. Farming wasn't my dish, so I pulled stakes when I was fifteen and headed west for here—Arizona. Been knocking around these parts ever since. You born in Ohio?"

Abby watched him blow a cloud of smoke into the motionless air and shook her head. "No—Indiana. It was when I married John that we moved to Ohio—and the farm."

Zell considered her in the soft, flickering glow of the fire. "You don't look like a farmer's wife to me. You're much too, well, I reckon the word's lovely."

Abby blushed for the third time, and laughed, a bright, happy sound in the hush. "Thank you for the compliment, Tom, but I am although, like you: I don't care for the life. Unlike you, I couldn't run away from it."

"Why not?"

Abby's shoulders stirred. "There are many things a man can do that a woman cannot. Usually we are thrust into something—a marriage perhaps—and there's no escape."

"Is that what's troubling you?"

She gave him a quick glance and then lowered her eyes. "I—I didn't realize that it showed that much."

"Hard to miss," Zell said. "I'm willing to listen if you're of a mind to talk. Helps sometimes to unload."

Abby shook her head. "No—but thanks. My prob-

lems are my own." She turned her eyes to where John
Nace was yet in conversation with Fisk and Tolan.
The women had cleared up the table, one made by
laying boards across two barrels, and would soon be
making preparations for bed.

"Will we have trouble crossing the desert?" Abby
asked then as if anxious to change the subject. Taking
up the pot of chicory, she raised her brows question-
ingly.

Tom waved the offer aside. He could stand a drink
of whiskey, were it handy, but he'd had enough of
the coffee substitute.

"Hard to say. Never know where the outlaw gangs
are hanging out, but I hope to dodge them. You have
any problems coming out from Ohio? It's a long
trip."

"Nothing serious. We left Independence with about
a dozen other wagons, and followed the Santa Fe
Trail until we got close to Colorado. They turned off
and went on then while we headed south—for California."

"Could have cut straight across, saved some miles."

"The men talked about doing that, but a man up
there warned us of snow—said it would catch us sure.
We were joined by two other parties at Santa Fe, but
they were going to El Paso, so we lost them, too, after
a time. The only trouble we've run into, or rather,
that we may have, will be after we leave here."

Darkness had closed in and full night, relieved only
by the flare of the fires, had claimed the camp. Zell,
puffing absently on his cigar, watched Abby Nace
through partly shut eyes. Whatever it was that lay between the woman and her husband was serious, and
he wondered again what it might be. Whatever, John

Nace was a fool; with a wife like Abby, an appreciative man would go out of his way to make her happy.

"Expect I'd better clear up the table," she said, rising. "It's getting late."

"I can help—"

"No. You sit right where you are. I'll warm up the coffee—"

"Never mind," Tom said, watching her quick, efficient movements as she gathered up the dishes and carried them to a pan of water at the edge of the fire.

He supposed he should be about making preparations for the morning departure—having his own look at the wagons and teams, making certain they were ready to roll, and checking the water kegs and such—but it was now too dark for a close inspection. Anyway, the party had come all the way from Ohio and, by now trail-wise, doubtless had long since learned to see to such matters.

"The nights are so warm and pleasant," he heard Abby say. "And beautiful, too. At times it seems like I could reach up and touch one of the stars."

Zell nodded, glanced to the sky. It was a soft black canopy studded with sparkling bits of silver. The moon, late in rising, was going to be bright and would add to the mellow glow that now covered the land. That was good; the train, once underway, could move at night if it became necessary.

Coming erect, Tom stepped back into the shadows alongside the Nace wagon, where he would be nearer to Abby as she cleaned her dishes. She was silent as she went about the task, and the fire's glow striking her intent features lent a sort of golden sheen to her skin. Again Zell thought of Nace and what a fool the man must be.

Abby, half turning at that moment, caught Tom

studying her, and smiled. "I'll be finished here in a minute or two, and—"

But Zell's attention was no longer on her as he raised a hand to still her voice. A dozen or so men were standing at the edge of the camp. They were barely visible in the pale flare of the flames.

9

"Stay here—close to the wagon," Zell murmured.

Abby, glancing at him, saw the direction into which he was looking and shifted her eyes to that point. Others in the camp had now become aware of the intruders and were facing them.

"Who are they?" Abby whispered.

Tom had been considering the men closely, wondering if it could be a party of Sackman's friends coming to even the score with him as Hannemeyer had prophesied. But they didn't appear to be working miners; they looked more the worthless trash that hung around the small, ragtag saloons hoping to catch some drunk unawares and strip him of his money and possessions.

"Bums," Zell replied, "and some of them will be busters—men who've gone broke at mining, lost everything, and now keep themselves by stealing and robbing folks who can't look out for themselves."

"But us—a wagon train—"

"Small outfit like this is what they like to find. It's made to order for them."

"Are they dangerous—I mean, would they kill?"

"Can bet on it. They'll take what they want, and anybody that tries to stop them had better be able to back his stand."

"What do you—" Abby began, and broke off as the renegades, having sized up the camp and taking note of the few men in attendance, moved in nearer.

Tom, standing in the deep shadows of the Naces' wagon, watched them narrowly. They were rough, unkempt men in ragged clothing, and all were armed.

"Well, would you looky here," one in the forefront called in a loud voice. "We've got us a whole passel of corn-shuckers—and they're just a-waiting to welcome us!"

A chorus of comment and laughter followed the leader's words as the renegades continued to advance.

"Hold it—right there," Caleb Tolan sang out abruptly, coming to his feet as he recognized danger. "What do you want?"

The outlaws slowed. The man in the front, a squat, heavily bearded individual in dirty overalls, checked shirt, and high-crowned hat, came to a halt. The boots he was wearing, partly visible, were a glossy black and looked to be new—taken no doubt off some luckless victim.

"What'd you say, grandpa?"

Fisk and Nace had joined Tolan, now stood at his side.

"Ask you what you was wanting—"

The heavyset man, glancing about at his followers, grinned broadly. "Well, just about everything you've got, I reckon—especially your women."

"Get out," Fisk shouted. "Move on or—"

"Or what? I don't see no iron in your hand, sodbuster. How you figure to make us trot?"

"Easy," Zell said, stepping out of the shadows. Pistol drawn, he placed a shot at the feet of the outlaw leader.

The man yelled, swore, and jumped back a step. "Who the hell you think you are—shooting at me—"

"I know who he is, Perch," one of the otulaws close by said loudly. "He's that gun-shark—the one I was telling you about. Was him that cut down them three jaspers in the saloon."

Perch drew himself fully erect and hung his hands on his hips. Thrusting his head forward, he grinned.

"So you're the big muckity-muck around here—the high-toned cock of the walk! Been hoping to run across you."

"Perch, you best shut up, back off—"

Tom remained motionless, a slack, nerveless figure in the half-light. The renegade carried two guns, he saw, one in a holster at his side, the other thrust into the left pocket of his overalls.

"Nope, I ain't about to back off," Perch declared. "Aim to pull the tail feathers out of this bird and then go right ahead and help myself to whatever I fancy."

"Better listen to your friend," Zell said in his quiet way. He was partly turned from the fire, thus preventing the glare from affecting his eyes, and at that angle his chiseled features were a soft-edged bronze.

"There's no cause for a shooting," John Nace said reasonably, taking a hand in the matter. "If it's food you men need, why, I expect we can spare you some. We won't turn anybody away hungry."

Perch laughed, but kept his eyes on Zell. "Done told you what we was after—and it sure ain't grub! We're wanting your money and your guns and them there gals—"

"Perch, we maybe ought to forget it."

The heavyset man wagged his shaggy head. "Nope, ain't going to. They's ten of us—and your fancy-shooting friend there's the only one with a gun. I'll take care of him and then this here outfit's ours—all of it."

Abruptly Tom Zell whipped up his pistol and fired. Perch yelled, clutched at his chest, and staggering back, fell to the ground.

A shout went up from the rest of the renegades. Zell took a quick step to one side, triggered his weapon again. He took no aim, simply shot into the ranks of the suddenly milling outlaws. A yell of pain sounded. Cool, Zell waited until the echo of the shot had faded and then, powder smoke hanging about him, fired once again, this time directing the bullet into the air.

"All of you," he called in a harsh voice. "I want you away from here in two minutes! Pick up your friend and move out. You try coming back and bothering these folks, I'll kill you like I did him."

The confusion slowed, ceased. Several of the renegades hastily turned, headed back for town. Others, four in number, came forward gingerly, paused beside Perch, their eyes on Zell as if half expecting to receive the same fate.

"Pick him up and get out of here," Tom snapped. "Getting tired of waiting on you!"

The men bent over at once. Each took the outlaw leader by a leg or arm, and straightening up, hurried off into the night toward the distant scatter of lights that was the town.

Rigid, not losing sight of the renegades for a moment, Zell removed the empties from his pistol and reloaded. And then, as the outlaws were lost in the darknesss, he came about, found that the homesteaders had gathered around him and were extending their thanks and congratulations.

"It's what you hired me for," he said, pride lifting within him. It was a new experience, something heretofore unknown. Shoot-outs prior to this had been to satisfy his ego and maintain his reputation; this one had been in defense of others.

"Well, we're sure thankful you was here," Cáleb Tolan declared. "Don't know what would have happened if you hadn't been."

Tom shrugged, turned his head, and caught Abby Nace's glance. A smile parted her lips as if she were taking a measure of pride from his actions, too, and that sent another unfamiliar but different feeling flowing through him.

"Chance we could've talked them out of whatever they wanted to do," he heard John Nace say. "Killing that fellow wasn't right. It was cold-blooded murder!"

"Don't be a fool, John," Fisk snapped. "We just had our first look at outlaws. They meant business!"

"Can bet on it," Zell said. "Talking would've been a waste of time."

"You shot him before he went for his gun. How do you know he would have used it? I thought there was some kind of a code between you shooters—that you always waited and—"

"Not when you're dealing with a bunch like that and the odds are all against you," Tom said, temper lifting slightly. In that moment he realized he didn't like John Nace, actually hadn't from the start, but just hadn't admitted it to himself.

"They're men," Nace said stubbornly. "I just won't believe they can't be reasoned with."

"Not that kind," Zell countered. "You—all of you—better get that straight in your heads. Things are a lot different out here. A bunch like that—renegades, saloon bums, busters, thieves—they all take what they want if they can, and they won't hold back on killing to do it."

"I believe it," Martha Fisk said. "The way they was looking things over—especially the girls."

A silence followed the elderly woman's words, as if all were suddenly aware of how near disaster they had been. Far off in the quiet night a coyote yipped, the sound starting a dog somewhere in the settlement to barking.

"Well, all I can say is we're mighty beholden to you, Tom, for taking over," Reuben Fisk said. "Can bet your bottom dollar that from here on out we're all going to be more careful."

"Be a good idea if you will all carry a gun, starting now," Zell said. "A sixshooter, if you've got one and can use it, or a rifle or shotgun. Makes no big difference to me which—just want you armed. Goes for you women, too. If you can shoot, keep a weapon handy."

"You think they'll come back?" Fisk asked.

"Doubt it, but it'll pay to set up a watch. Each of us can take a couple of hours."

"I'll go first," George Tolan offered.

Zell glanced at the young man, heretofore a silent figure staying strictly in the shadows of his elders. It was as if the danger to Purity that the outlaws posed had crystallized his manhood and made him conscious of the responsibilities he must assume.

"Good," Zell said, finding himself liking the boy. He pointed to a clump of mesquite beyond the reach of the fire. "Take a stand over there. You can see anybody coming up to camp, but they won't spot you. I'll spell you in a couple of hours."

"And I'll spell you," Fisk said. "Caleb, it'll be up to

you to take over from me, then it'll be Nace's turn. Ought to be about time to pull out after that."

"Should be," Zell agreed. "Be a smart idea if we all, except George, will turn in now and get some rest. Figure to start by first light, and that means we're up and about an hour before that. . . . And keep your guns handy," he added as he turned, moved off toward the spot where he'd laid his gear.

"Good night," several voices called to him. He replied, but his attention was on Abby Nace. Her lips were parted in that now-familiar and welcome smile; as their eyes met, she nodded.

"Good night," he said in words meant only for her ears, and continued on his way.

10

Purity Fisk, sitting on a stool near the dying fire as she braided her blond hair, stared dreamily out across the low, starlit hills. She and Patience were the only ones still not in their beds—this night to be with their parents inside the wagon instead of beneath it. There was just a possibility, it was thought, that the outlaws would come back and Martha Fisk was taking no chances with her girls.

"Did you see how he looked when he stepped out of the shadows and stopped those—those outlaws? He was like some kind of avenging angel."

Patience, also preparing her thick tresses for the night, paused, frowned. Her younger sister worried her. Ever since Tom Zell had ridden into camp, Purity had been in a sort of glowing trance. Time after time she had mentioned his arrival—how he sat his saddle, so erect and square-shouldered; the way he wore his hat tipped forward over his hard-cut, almost-savage face; his pale eyes, which seemed to drill right through a person as if trying to learn that person's thoughts.

And now Purity had a new vision to revel in—the way he had faced up to all those outlaws and calmly shot and killed the leader to stop them from coming into the camp.

54

Patience had been thrilled, too—right from the start—by Tom Zell, and she'd immediately had ideas about him . . . and her. Age was creeping up on her steadily; she was now almost twenty, with no prospects of a husband, and the thought was most unsettling. She really should sort of take matters in hand, set her cap—

"Do you suppose he's all those wicked things that John Nace told Papa about?" Purity wondered.

"I expect so," Patience replied, resuming her braiding.

The younger girl shivered. "Wouldn't it be something to be married to him! I can just imagine what it would be like, so thrilling, so—so desperate and—"

"You better stop all that moon-calfing over him," Patience said sternly. "You're forgetting that you're going to marry George Tolan."

"Oh, fiddle-de-dee on George! He's an old stick-in-the-mud. You take him!"

Patience considered her young sister thoughtfully. She wasn't certain that Purity meant what she'd said, but it instilled a glimmer of hope. Maybe, if things did work out between Purity and Tom Zell—leaving George free—there might be a chance for her with him.

"I—I wish it was that easy," she murmured.

The comment was lost on Purity. She continued to gaze off into the soft, bright night oblivious to everything, even to the yapping of coyotes gathered not far from the camp. Intelligent as well as wary, the sly little desert wolves had learned that the leavings of travelers always afforded not only good but easy bounty.

"You should stop flirting with him," Patience said then, torn between her duty as an older sister and per-

sonal needs. "I watched you, slanting your eyes at him
and twisting yourself about like—like some street
hussy."

Charity turned to her impulsively. "Do you think
he noticed me?"

"Of course he did. A man like him never misses
anything like that."

Purity's voice had a breathless quality. "Then do
you think he's interested in me?"

"Now, how would I know that?" Patience demanded bluntly. "Can tell you this, he had an eye on
Abby Nace—and she was sure letting him know he
was welcome."

Purity's features clouded. "I think Abby was just
being nice when she asked him to take supper with
them."

"Everybody asked him, but you notice where he
went."

The younger girl gave that thought. "Was she really bold? I mean, was Abby actually—"

"I'm afraid so. Something's happened between her
and John. They act like they hardly know each other
anymore."

"I know. I heard Mama and Lydia talking about
them. But I don't think Abby would up and do anything like going off with Tom Zell, do you?"

"I'd not be surprised. I think she'd go the limit to
get him—"

"Well, she can just forget about it. If it takes going
to bed with him to—"

"Girls!" Martha Fisk called from the wagon. "You
should be asleep. Now, both of you, get in here at
once!"

"Yes, Mama," Patience answered, rising. Turning,

she waited for her sister to come to her feet also. "Do you mean that?"

Eyes dancing, Purity nodded. "I'll do what I have to," she said, and then hesitating, caught at Patience's arm. "You won't tattle to Mama, will you? Please?"

The older girl shrugged. It had been a pact between them ever since they were small. "Of course not, but you best be careful, Purity. You could find yourself in bad trouble."

"I know, I know," Purity said, giggling, and hurried on.

Abby Nace lay quietly in bed beside her husband, John, wide awake and staring up at the white canvas arching over them. They had retired well over an hour ago and John, as usual, had immediately gone to sleep.

But such was not for her. Abby's mind was in turmoil, filled with the remembrance of Tom Zell, his actions, his words, and the way he had looked at her, so direct, so brazenly wanting.

And, heaven help her, she had similar feelings! It had been months now, long before they had departed their Ohio farm since she and John had been as husband and wife should be. Just what had come between them she could not recall, and she doubted John could either, but it was there, a high barrier shutting them one from the other, blocking off communication as effectively as if both had been struck deaf and dumb.

She had tried to cope with it, but failed, mostly, she felt, because her husband had made no similar effort. And then finally she had given up and resigned herself to the loneliness that was the natural progeny of neglect and indifference.

Why couldn't she have met Tom Zell, or a man like him, earlier—before she'd become acquainted with John Nace and married him? Zell would have given her the love and attention she longed for and brought excitement and adventure into her life.

She could imagine what it would be like married to him—a gambler, hard drinker, gunman and killer, a woman-chaser, and all such traits that society frowned upon. Perhaps he would be difficult to live with, not because he liked women—she could handle that by simply making herself so compliant and desirable that he'd have no other needs.

But the rest could pose a problem. Gamblers, she'd heard, were most always broke. It was like a horrible disease, folks said, and the family of such a man suffered terribly.

Liquor, too, could be a curse and was known to be the cause of much grief and trouble. There had been hardly any drinking in her father's house, and John was a teetotaler, at least insofar as she knew, thus a man who drank heavily would take some getting used to—but she'd be willing to assume the risk and try and live with the problem if it meant Tom Zell.

Being a gunman—one who hired out to protect folks, even to the point of killing other men—was something else she would need to accept and adjust to, but she believed it possible. The hardest part would be the worry involved, the times when she would wonder if he was coming back to her alive or if she would get word of him lying dead somewhere in a pool of blood. But that was hardly possible and there was small chance of it ever happening. He was, according to all she'd heard, too expert for that to overtake him.

Abby stirred restlessly, remembering once again the way Zell had looked at her when he rode in, the way he had faced those outlaws—so quiet and sure, the absolute power and strength that radiated from him reaching out and having its reassuring effect upon all the others.

And most of all the attention he had given her. She'd endeavored not to show her reactions, but knew she had failed miserably, and now those moments, swollen by recollection, were haunting her relentlessly.

Brushing aside the light coverlets, Abby sat up. She could find no rest, but such might come if she rose, walked about for a bit, and settled her nerves.

"John," she murmured, laying a hand on his shoulder and shaking it gently.

He half-rolled toward her. "Yes?"

"I can't sleep. I'm getting up for a few minutes."

He made no reply and, uncaring, turned back onto his side and resumed his slumber. Abby, pulling herself to her knees, made her way to the wagon's tailgate, and drawing about her shoulders the spare blanket at the foot of their bed, she dropped lightly to the ground.

Pausing there long enough to pull on a pair of knitted slippers, she moved slowly off into the silvery night, her feet making soft, padding noises on the sun-baked ground.

Circling the wagon, Abby glanced to where the Fisks had halted their vehicle. All appeared quiet and serene. The same was true where the Tolans were concerned. She remembered George at that moment. He was acting as a guard, keeping a watch for those outlaws in the event they returned. Looking closely, she could make out his hunched figure in the deep shadows of the mesquite tree where Tom Zell had suggested he sit.

Tom Zell . . . without conscious thought Abby came about and retraced her steps and walked to where she could see him stretched out in the blankets he'd laid within a half-circle of some brush. Breath tight in her throat, she halted beside him.

He was sleeping soundly, face turned from her; with the light from the moon and stars pointing up his hard-cut profile, Abby had her first uninhibited look at him.

For several minutes she stood there staring down at him, at the man she wished she might call her own, hoping that he might awaken and see her, silently praying that he would not; and then wheeling slowly, she returned to the wagon and her bed.

11

They were well on their way by the appointed hour that next morning, and by the time sunlight was flooding across the flats and racing down the dark slopes, the train had settled into a steady pace.

Zell was taking a northwesterly course from Wickenburg, one that skirted the settlement and decreased the possibility of their passage being noted. It was only a faint, seldom-used trail that wound its way through the low hills, but as Zell had explained to Fisk and the others, it would take them a considerable distance from the usual course followed by pilgrims, and thus the possibility of their encountering one of the various bands of outlaws would be greatly reduced.

"We'll be heading for the Santa Maria River," he said as, with the Naces, he partook of a hearty breakfast of corn cakes, bacon, and chicory coffee. "Means we'll bypass the Harcuvar Mountains and have pretty fair going for a while."

"It much out of the way to swing north?" Fisk wanted to know.

"Some," Zell admitted, "but you're hiring me to get you to the Colorado River with a whole skin. Best way to do that is stick to the back roads."

The main route would have been much easier, the tracks having been pounded into hard-surfaced lanes by the countless wagons and stagecoaches and other traffic that pursued that course, but Tom felt there was no cause for worry on that score.

Earlier he'd had a close look at the Ohio party's equipment. All of the wagons had been thoroughly reinforced before getting underway and were, as a result, still in good condition. The teams also were in excellent shape and, most of all, would be equal to the task that lay ahead.

Caleb Tolan had mules—four big husky brutes, two of which he trailed while driving their counterparts. Fisk, with a pair each of horses and mules, followed a like alternating procedure. Nace, with a lighter wagon, had but one span of horses, but they were tough Morgan geldings, strong and tireless, and it was doubtful they'd come up against anything they could not master.

All else met his approval, too, for thanks to the many miles that lay between the Ohio River and the town of Wickenburg, all deficiencies and problems pertaining to such had been experienced and corrected.

As the day warmed, the pace slowed just as Zell had anticipated. There was little shade from the sun, vegetation running mostly to cactus, desert broom, snakeweed, creosote bush, mesquite, and the like, but he heard no complaints from the pilgrims although he dropped back periodically from his position a quarter-mile or so ahead of the train to assure himself that all was well.

While he had no particular fear of encountering Apaches in the area, and even less outlaws, who were more inclined to lurk along the more-frequented main roads, Zell still maintained a sharp watch for any dust that would indicate the presence of riders.

The yellowish pall the train was stirring up, while

thin, would be seen for miles through the clear, desert air and he knew such would attract Indian hunting parties and bands of outlaws should they be around. It was a matter of pure luck, Tom felt, and hoped that it would smile upon him and his charges.

They rested around midday, halting in a shallow wash along which several paloverde trees grew. Most found it too hot to eat and sought only to get out of their wagons and enjoy the light if barely cool breeze drifting in from the mountains far to the north.

"How long will it take us to reach that river you told us about?"

Tom, standing at the side of his bay horse, having a drink from the bottle in his saddlebags, came about slowly. It was the youngest daughter of the Fisks— Purity. She was regarding him with a pretty smile.

"Should get there by tomorrow night if we don't run into bad luck," he replied, corking the liquor and shoving it back into the leather pouch. The sight of his drinking had brought no frown of disapproval to the girl's features, he noted, but had instead seemed to meet with approval, as if she considered it a mark of stature.

"Bad luck—by that you mean outlaws or maybe Indians?"

Purity was just making conversation, Zell knew. He had been all through the matter earlier that day, but he nodded and gave her the serious attention he would grant any of the others.

"Not so much them, but an accident—a wheel breaking, one of the wagons overturning or maybe getting stuck in the sand—"

"Purity! Mama wants you—"

At the sound of her sister's voice, the girl glanced

quickly over her shoulder. A faint glow suffused her skin and annoyance sparkled in her brown eyes.

"Oh, fiddle," she muttered, and then coming back around to Tom, said, "It was nice talking to you and I hope we can get together again tonight. There's a lot I want to ask you about."

"I'll be handy," Zell said, studying her closely. She was the one, he thought, that he'd been told was to marry George Tolan once they reached their new homes in California. Or did he have it wrong? Was it the other girl—Patience? This one acted as free and unfettered as a saloon girl.

Looking up at the sun to judge the hour, Tom swung into the saddle and gave the signal to move out. Then, raking the bay lightly with his spurs, he started forward to take up his place as outrider, purposely veering close to the Nace wagon, which was bringing up the rear.

Abby's eyes met his as he passed, and she was smiling. He responded with a fingertip to the brim of his flat-crowned hat—all of which went unnoticed by John Nace.

But earlier that previous night such had not been the case. He had been aware of her coming to where he lay, feigning sleep. The sound of someone approaching, while quiet, had not escaped his danger-honed senses and he had carefully turned to see who it might be. He caught sight of Nace watching from the back of his wagon at the same moment he saw Abby and accordingly gave no sign that he knew of her presence.

The heat increased as the afternoon wore on, but it was mild compared to what it would be a month from then, Zell assured Martha Fisk when mention was made of the fact; the woman and the others appeared to take comfort from the thought.

Tom, although preferring to continue after sunset, when the land was beginning to cool, called a halt while there was still an hour until the day was over. They had traveled fairly far that first day, one during which they'd had their initial taste of the true desert—which all had weathered well—and it was only right they pull up early and make camp.

He chose a level place on the opposite bank of a wide and somewhat deep arroyo and there had the wagons pulled into a triangular formation. No sooner had the arrangement been completed when Fisk and Nace came to him.

"Me and John was wondering if it wouldn't be better to camp down in the wash," Fisk said. "If the wind gets up, it won't hit us down there."

"Nobody'll see us, either," Nace added.

Zell shook his head. "Too risky. This time of the year we could get hit by a flash flood, and if it came in the middle of the night, it'd wipe us out."

"Flood?" Reuben Fisk echoed, glancing up at the sky. "Hell, there ain't a cloud in sight!"

"Makes no difference around here. Rain could hit ten miles up the way and we'd not know about it. But we would when the water came pouring down this arroyo. It's a big one, probably a hundred smaller ones empty into it between here and those mountains you see off to the north."

Fisk mopped at the sweat on his face and neck with a bandanna. "Well, I reckon you know best."

"I do," Zell said dryly. "Make your cook fires down in the wash where they won't show—and keep them small."

"Thought you said that by us coming this roundabout way we'd not run into trouble," Nace said, frowning.

"Nothing's ever for sure," Tom said, and moved on.

Later, after the evening meal was over, Zell, having—at Purity's insistence—eaten with the Fisks, set the night watch, dividing as before the time equally between the four men and himself. All were bone-tired from the long, hot day, and not so much as an act of kindness but as a matter of precaution, he assigned the first shift to himself, certain that any one of the others without a bit of prior rest, would doze.

Personally, he felt little effect from the day. Accustomed to the heat and the saddle, he was aware of only a normal amount of weariness, and after fortifying himself with a good drink from his bottle, he took up his rifle and climbed to a low rise a hundred feet or so from the wagons.

Most of the pilgrims were crawling into their beds as he started up the gentle grade, and by the time he had made himself comfortable, all, he suspected, were asleep.

That was a relief. He could now relax and enjoy the quiet. It was his kind of night, he thought; fresh-smelling, with the land all silver and shadow under a sky littered with stars and a bright moon. A bird called softly from somewhere along the arroyo, one of the horses stamped restlessly, and far off to the east in the direction of the Date Creek hills, coyotes were tuning up.

Taking a cigar from the case, Tom bit off its end, and carefully cupping a match, thumbnailed it into life and lit the weed. Exhaling a cloud of smoke, he then settled back, his thoughts going at once to Abby Nace and on to young Purity Fisk. He was uncertain just how to figure the girl; if she were the one slated to marry George Fisk, it looked to him as if there was something wrong; with her bold, forward attitude, she was certainly asking for attention of the most personal kind—and that was far removed from what a person would expect of a soon-to-be bride.

Abby Nace was a different matter. A full-grown woman, married, acquainted with life and its complexities, Tom had no doubt she was completely aware of herself and the consquences of anything she might do. But he was still unable to understand the nature of the Naces' problem. Why would John let a beautiful woman like Abby, his wife—

Zell drew up sharply. Movement near the Tolan wagon had caught his attention. Laying the cigar aside, he took up his rifle, and eyes on a dark, indefinite figure now coming toward him, he waited, straining to make out who it was. That it was no outsider he could be sure; he would have seen whoever it was coming out of the arroyo.

"Tom—"

Zell propped the rifle against the clump of broom beside him, retrieved his cigar, and settled back. It was Abby Nace.

"Here," he replied.

12

Zell watched as Abby climbed the gentle slope to where he sat. Clad in a white, quilted robe, dark hair hanging loosely about her shoulders, face a pale oval in the soft light, she looked more an apparition than a warm woman of flesh and blood.

"I couldn't sleep," she said. "Do you mind if I sit with you for a while?"

"My pleasure," Zell replied, preparing a place at his side for her.

Abby came forward at once, and gathering the robe about herself, sat down beside him. Gazing out over the soft-edged hills and flats, she shook her head.

"I can't get over how beautiful the nights are out here. It's hard to realize it's the same country in the daytime. It looks so harsh, so forbidding then."

"I reckon it's all in how you see it," Tom said, blowing a small cloud of smoke into the motionless, warm air and watching it slowly drift away. "To me there's nothing like it—I could never get used to anything else."

"I think I can understand. The desert has a hard kind of beauty, a sort of grandeur I guess you'd call it, or maybe the word should be majestic."

"Whatever, it's a dangerous place, too," Zell said. "It can kill you if you aren't careful."

"I know," Abby murmured, and fell silent.

Away from the wagon, from the others in the party, she was a different woman, Tom thought: friendly, talkative, and altogether at ease.

"I envy you being a part of all this," she said after a time. "You seem so free, so far from the grinding way of life that I'm familiar with."

Zell gave that consideration, found deeper meaning in her words. "Was it always that way—right from the start?"

Abby, hands clasped in her lap, continued to stare off into the distance. The coyotes were in full chorus by then, and off in the not too far distance, a solitary wolf added his lonely howl.

"No, I suppose not—if you mean when I was first married. John and I were happy in the beginning."

"Works that way sometimes—"

"He's a good man, a fine one, really, and when we started out, he had high hopes—dreams I guess you could call them. We were going to have the best farm along the Ohio—one that would not only make us a good living but would provide us with enough extra money to go into business.

"John has always wanted to own a store—and he still does. He says there's a lot of money in supplying folks with the things they have to have, and if a person can find the right location, one where you have the only store for miles around, you can actually get rich."

Abby paused. Zell removed the stogie from his mouth and glanced at her. She was still looking off into the night, but now a deep loneliness had claimed her features.

"He worked so hard and the first year or two we did pretty good. Then the next season the river came out of its banks and washed away our crop and ruined everything. We had some money put aside—it was to be used to start our store—and John used that the next spring to start over. It wasn't a good year. We barely made enough to get by on."

"Odds against ever making it big in farming always looked too high to me," Zell said. "I figure a man's chances are better at a poker table or bucking the tiger."

Abby nodded. "Anything's better than farming," she said wearily. "We did good that next season, but then the one after that—last year—when things were doing fine and we stood to recover all we'd lost, the river wiped us out again. We lost everything—even the house. It had to be torn down.

"It was terrible what it did to John. He became bitter and withdrawn and lost all interest in life. When our neighbors, the Tolans and the Fisks, decided to give up and head west, I got him to agree to go along. At that time I don't think he had it in mind to start over, I believe it was more because he was at loose ends and didn't know what to do.

"But now I know it went deeper than that; he had just given up on everything—even us. We drifted apart, and before I realized it or could try to do anything about it, we became like two strangers, going days and nights sometimes with hardly a word spoken between us. He just shut me and the rest of the world out."

"Must've been plenty lonesome for you—"

"It was—more than you can imagine. We didn't have many friends, just about none, in fact. John is not the friendly sort and folks never took to him much. The Fisks and the Tolans are about the only ones, and they never have been close."

"Don't know much about such things, but seems to me if you'd had a couple of—"

"We tried," Abby cut in despondently, "but something was wrong. We just couldn't have children—and that was another big disappointment to John. I'm sure things would have worked out differently if we could have had a son or a daughter, but life failed him there, too, he feels."

Abby hesitated, turned suddenly to Tom Zell. He thought she was going to mention the previous night when she had come to where he lay, and believing him to be asleep, turned away. But he was wrong.

"I'm talking too much—way too much. I know I must be boring you."

"Nope, I'm a listener—always have been—and I'm pleased to know you trust me enough to unload what's on your mind."

Abby leaned forward impulsively as if to kiss him, caught herself, and drew back. "It helps so to talk to someone. I've had all this backed up inside me for so long that, well, it's been like a wall of water just straining to break loose."

"Said yesterday you'd sold your land—you and the others. It hurt much to part with it?"

"Some. We'd lived there for several years and had put a lot of ourselves into it, but I don't miss it now. We took part of the money we got for it, bought the wagon and team we're using, along with some necessities. The rest we're keeping to pay off the balance on our land in California and start over again."

"Your husband still hoping to go into business?"

"Yes, I think so, but it's not like it was before. Something's gone out of his dream. He doesn't live for it like he did back in Ohio before we lost everything. He just sort of accepts the idea but makes no big plans, as if he'd lost all faith in the future.

"I feel the same. What lies ahead for me is a void—like trying to look into a room filled with darkness. And I don't care. John and I mean nothing to each other, my family back in Indiana is gone: my parents both dead and my sister and brother moved away and perhaps dead, too. I'm nothing more than a leaf floating in a stream, drifting along, going nowhere and unable to do anything about it."

Zell removed the cigar from his mouth and glanced at its lifeless tip. Tossing it off into the brush, he half-turned, put his arm around the woman, and drawing her close, kissed her. She did not resist; instead, sighing contentedly, she went limp in his embrace. For a time they sat quietly in the shadow of the brush, and then, disengaging herself, Abby pulled back from him. Zell started to speak, but she laid a finger against his lips, silencing him.

"Don't say anything. I just want to sit here and think—and remember. It's the first time I've felt a man's arms about me, or been kissed, in years. I'm what folks call a neglected wife."

Tom swore softly. "Can't figure your husband! With a wife like you any man I know would give up everything he had to keep her—make her happy."

She smiled at him. "I know it's a foolish thing to say, but I wish it had been you that I met and married, and not John."

"Afraid I've got too many drawbacks to make any woman a good husband—"

"Perhaps, but you do have the things that are important. Drawbacks, as you call them, don't really count. Two people in love marry despite such things—it's the feeling they have for each other that matters. . . . Haven't you ever been married?"

"Nope, just never felt the need or—"

"I've heard," Abby cut in. "You've got plenty of lady friends, some—according to John—that you'll kill for."

"Most of what's been said about me has been stretched a mile, I'm afraid. Best you don't believe everything you hear."

"I don't mind—it doesn't offend me. In fact, I've wondered what it would be like to be married to you, just what sort of a life it would be, I mean."

"Not good," Tom said flatly. "I'm not the kind to settle down."

"Even if you found the right woman?"

Zell pushed back his hat, rubbed at his jaw thoughtfully. More coyotes had joined the desert chorus and the night was now filled with their discordant music.

"Not sure I'd know it—if and when I did," he said in absolute honesty.

"You'd know," Abby assured him. "Even if there's been many others, you'd know. There's a magic something inside you that tells you—I realize that now. Haven't you ever felt it?"

He shook his head. "Can't say that I have."

Abby shrugged, and gathering the robe about her, started to get up. "I'd best be getting back to the wagon."

Zell nodded. "Probably. Fisk'll be here pretty quick to spell me," he said, and coming to his feet, took her by the hand and helped her rise. "Finding you here with me in nothing but a nightgown and a robe would make it bad for you."

She turned to him. "It doesn't matter—let them think what they want. . . . Thank you, Tom, for listening to my troubles and, well, for being understanding. Good night."

" 'Night," Zell replied, and watched her walk slowly back toward the wagons.

Abby had said nothing about her one-sided visit to him that night before, evidently having a reason for not doing so. Respecting her decision, he had remained silent about it also.

13

A heavy stillness, like a premonition, hung over the desert that next morning as the wagons prepared to move out. It laid an uneasiness over the party; and as Caleb Tolan, in the lead wagon, waited impatiently for Fisk, who was that day to bring up the rear, to get his vehicle into place, he beckoned to Zell.

"What's this mean?" he asked when Tom had ridden in alongside. "Back home we'd be looking for a tornado."

"We'll be getting some wind all right," Zell replied. "Hard to figure how bad it'll be."

"You get tornadoes out here?"

"I've never seen one, but things can get plenty wild."

A shout from Fisk announced his readiness, and Zell, pulling away from Tolan, spurred on ahead. He had altered course, was choosing a more westerly direction. They were well clear of the Harcuvars now and it would save time and miles to get on a direct route for the Santa Maria River.

He looked back. The wagons had strung out behind him, their iron-tired wheels making harsh, grating sounds as they sliced through the sand while the hooves of the horses thudded softly with each step. There was no conversation between the pilgrims at that early hour and Tom guessed all but the drivers had gone back to sleep.

As the sun broke over the horizon to the east, Zell turned his attention to the sky. A yellowish haze hovered over the desert and was growing in depth. Tom swore softly. They were in for wind, that was certain, and with it sand and dust. How soon there was no way of knowing, but he reckoned he'd best warn the pilgrims. Wheeling the bay around, he cut back to the lead wagon.

George had taken over the team, was sitting forward, elbows on knees, lines hanging slack from his thick fingers. Caleb was beside him, puffing contentedly on his pipe and rocking gently with the motion of the wagon. Lydia was not to be seen.

"Looks like that wind we were talking about's on the way," he said, jerking a thumb toward the east.

Both men turned, considered the pall. Caleb removed the pipe from his mouth. "Something we can do about it?"

"Not much, being out on the flat like we are. Will be a good idea to tie down everything loose so you won't lose it. If the sand gets too bad, I'll look for a place where we can pull up—a deep wash or a thick stand of brush—and wait until it's over."

"Can you say how soon it'll hit? Looks pretty far off," George said.

Zell shook his head. "No way to figure, but I'd guess it'll hit us about the middle of the morning. Could change directions, shift, miss us altogether."

There was little hope of that, Tom knew as he rode on, but he had seen it happen, and there was always a chance there could be a repeat. Reaching the Nace wagon, he repeated his warning to John, alone on the seat. The homesteader signified his understanding with a bob of his head, preferring to make no audible comment and keep his eyes straight ahead. Abby, Zell supposed, like Lydia Tolan, was back in the wagon and probably asleep.

Was Nace aware of Abby's visit to him while he was on watch that night before—as he was of the first time? Tom wondered as he moved on. The homesteader had said nothing of it, which was what could ordinarily be expected under the circumstances, but John Nace was a strange one, and hard to figure out.

It was different at the Fisk wagon. Both Reuben and Martha were on the seat now and their two daughters were at their shoulders. A lively conversation appeared to be in progress as Zell approached. It ceased at once when he reined in.

"Looks like we're in for a blow," Tom said, and repeated again the information and suggestion he'd given Tolan and Nace.

Reuben, with a pipe clamped between his teeth also, grinned. "Expect we can handle it. I've learned there ain't much a man can't take if he makes up his mind."

"You're right," Zell said, and started to pull away.

"It was nice having you eat with us last night," Purity said.

"Was my pleasure," he replied, smiling.

"Then maybe you'd like to do it again tonight. We're going to have—"

"Never you mind, young lady," Martha cut in sharply. "It's the Tolan's turn—and Lydia's already made plans."

"Not if he prefers to be with us—"

Zell shook his head. He would prefer taking his meals at Abby's table alone, but the alternating arrangement had been established and he felt he should abide by it.

"Obliged to you for the offer, but I reckon I best go where I'm expected," he said, eyes on Purity, and touching the brim of his hat, rode on.

The storm began late in the morning. At first there was a faint stirring of the broom and snakeweed and the infrequent stands of mesquite and similar larger shrubs. A soft whispering began to fill the darkening air. The sound gradually grew louder as the breeze gathered strength, and then, abruptly, a wind was upon them in full force.

Zell, only a short distance ahead and to the left of the Tolan wagon, felt the first blast of sand hit him broadside. Reaching for his neckerchief, he pulled it up over his mouth and nose, and halting, waited for the train to draw abreast. As he watched, the wind caught something from the Nace wagon—a bit of cloth or paper, he could not be sure which—and whirled it off into void. He had a quick glimpse of Abby's strained features as she peered out of the rear of the vehicle, and raising a hand, he waved, endeavoring to reassure her.

Waiting until the Fisks had rumbled by, Tom swung in behind, wanting to have his look at all three wagons and the trailing horses and mules to be certain all was well. He could find nothing to cause worry, and pulling his hat lower over his forehead to protect his eyes as much as possible, rode on.

Purity called something to him from the arched opening at the back of the Fisk wagon as he passed by, but the howling wind caught her words, whipped them away, and they were lost to him.

The blow increased with each minute, and as it rose, it became heavier with sand, dust, and fragments of dead weeds and such. Visibility shortened to only a few yards and the teams began to falter, both breath-

ing and sight impaired by the stinging particles of
sand and dust. He would have to find a shelter of
sorts where they could get out of the punishing blasts
soon, Tom realized.

But where? The desert was a broad flat in that particular area, broken only by low hills occasionally,
and that offered no protection at all. And because of
limited vision it was not possible to see for any distance and locate any larger formations. The world
had simply closed in about them, leaving them totally
isolated—but Zell knew it was up to him to find relief,
somewhere.

Hunched low over his saddle, head down, and quar-
tering the bay against the constant violence of the
wind, Tom moved out in front of the wagons. There
should be an arroyo nearby that would offer them
protection; or there could be a cluster of mesquite or
paloverde trees, or a hill high enough to have a lee
side. But an hour later, with the storm showing no
signs of decreasing, he was still searching.

Dropping back to the wagons, he signaled for a
halt. "See to your horses," he advised each as he rode
by, voice raised to be heard. "Dust'll be caked in their
nostrils. Clean them with a wet rag. Won't hurt to
wipe their eyes."

They were people accustomed to caring for stock,
he knew, but likely these were conditions they'd
never before encountered and he felt it only smart to
tell them what should be done.

When he had finished at the Fisk wagon, he swung
in behind it and dismounted. Taking a piece of cloth
from his saddlebags, he soaked it with water from his
canteen and set to work on the bay. That done, he
turned then to the team being trailed by Reuben, a
span of mules, and began to attend them. Almost im-

mediately he became aware that he was not alone. Glancing around, he saw Purity, a wet rag in her hand, dabbing at the off mules' nostrils. She smiled, said something.

"What?" Zell shouted.

The girl moved closer to him. "I said this was a terrible wind!"

He nodded, resumed working over the mule. After a moment he felt a hand on his arm.

"I'm thankful you're here," Purity shouted. "I don't know what I—we'd do if—if—"

"Part of the job," Zell replied.

"I know, but it's more than that to me. I feel safe, like everything will be all right."

"It will," Tom assured her, finished with the mule. Bowed against the driving gale, he turned, moved to the other; Purity had done but little to relieve the patient animal. Saying nothing, Zell began to wipe at its nostrils, mouth, and finally its eyes. That done, he crossed to his own horse.

"Expect I best give the Tolans a hand—"

"They'll be all right," Purity declared. "There's two of them."

"Need to go on, anyway. I'm looking for a place to pull up where we can get out of this wind."

"Everything all right back here?" Reuben Fisk called, suddenly appearing at the rear of his wagon.

"Mules are fine," Zell answered, swinging up onto his saddle. "I'm riding ahead. Still looking for spot to call a halt."

"Luck," Fisk shouted back as Tom moved off into the swirling haze.

Nace had apparently seen to his team and was standing beside them as Zell passed. The homesteader gave no sign of recognition; and Tom, glancing beyond him to Abby, crouched behind the seat in the protection of the canvas top, which was heaving wildly, nodded.

Purity Fisk had been right. Caleb had looked to the care of the team pulling the wagon while George had seen to the pair that were being trailed. Both men climbed up onto the seat as Tom came alongside.

"Hell, ain't it?" the elder Tolan remarked, brushing at the grit on his face. "Ain't never seen the beat of it!"

"It's a bad one for sure," Zell agreed, and pointed ahead. "Keep moving same direction. I'll find a place where we can stop sooner or later."

"We still a piece from that river?"

"Quite a ways," Tom said, and rode on.

14

An hour or so later, with the gusts of sand and dust-laden wind hammering at him relentlessly, Tom Zell reached a fairly wide arroyo that fulfilled his needs. Rushing water during rainstorms in the past had sliced a channel along its east bank to a depth that would furnish shelter from the blow.

Doubling back up the wash until he found a point where the teams and wagons could enter, Zell retraced his course to the train and led it to the haven.

Parking the wagons close to the arroyo's east wall, Tom and the other men made the horses and mules as comfortable as possible by swinging them about and placing their heads to the wall, where their eyes, mouths, and nostrils were out of reach of the wind. The upper half of the wagons' tops rose above the rim of the wash and the gale tore at the tough canvas with unabated fury, but there was nothing to be done about it.

As if called, the pilgrims all gravitated to the lead wagon, where they gathered around Caleb and Lydia Tolan. Sand and dust rimmed their lips and inflamed eyes, and they all had taken on a grayish color.

"Man'd think this dang wind would've blowed itself out by now," Tolan said in the comparative quiet of the arroyo. He had a wet cloth provided by Lydia in his hand and was wiping at his face. "These storms usually last this long?"

"I've seen them go for several days and nights with hardly a letup," Zell said, "and then they can die in only a couple of hours. I think this one's starting to quit."

The day had brightened somewhat, as if the sand and dust had thinned, and while there was still no blue sky visible, it seemed clearer overhead.

More wet cloths appeared and the pilgrims fell to removing the coating of grit they had accumulated. Tom, his attention turned to Abby and hopeful of an opportunity to speak with her, came about as he felt a wet cloth pressed into his hand.

"I thought you might like to wash off, too," Purity said, smiling.

She had cleaned her own features, even to having unfastened the top button of her dress and wiping well down on her breasts, both of which were now generously displayed. With a scarf holding her light hair in place, she looked to be little worse for the experience of the past few hours.

"Never know you'd been through a sandstorm," Tom said, starting to use the toweling.

Purity smiled again. "Here, let me do that for you," she said abruptly, and taking the cloth from him, began to cleanse his face. "Why, your mustache is chock-full of sand and dust!"

"Happens ever now and then," Zell said, looking beyond the girl to Abby. She was standing beside Martha Fisk, watching with no sign of expression. It was different where George Tolan was concerned. A dark frown knotted his forehead and narrowed his eyes as he looked on.

"It must have been terrible out there on your horse!

At least we had the wagon to sort of protect us, although I thought a couple of times that the wind was going to tear off the top."

Zell nodded, only half hearing as he listened to the wind. It still moaned and whistled wildly and a fine cloud of dust mixed with sand was continuing to sift down from the lip of the arroyo and settle on everything below, but there was no doubt the storm was diminishing.

"Don't you think I'm as pretty as Abby Nace?"

Zell came to attention, startled by Purity's blunt, unexpected question. She had evidently noticed him looking at Abby.

"Well, yes—I expect so," he replied, at a bit of a loss.

Purity had stepped back, was examining him critically. "Are you gone on her?"

Tom smiled at the expression. "She's a fine woman—"

"But I'm younger, and I've never been married," Purity stated boldly. "Doesn't that make you want me more than her?"

Zell stared at the girl for a long moment, thankful that they were beyond earshot of the others.

"I know I want you," she continued calmly.

Zell shrugged. Although accustomed to being surprised by the actions and words of women encountered in saloons, Purity's frankness had rocked him back on his heels. This, he supposed, was the talk that she had mentioned they would have that previous night but that somehow had gotten sidetracked—possibly when Abby Nace had come to sit with him while he was on guard.

"That's the wrong kind of talk to come from a girl who's about to be married," he said.

"Oh, that! I've changed my mind. I'm not going to get married—at least not to George Tolan. Do you want to know why?"

Abby had turned away, Tom noted, and was talking with Martha Fisk. He'd been right about which of the Fisk girls young Tolan was to marry; it was Purity and not her sister, Patience.

"No, sure don't. George is a fine man."

"I suppose he is, but he's not for me. I want a man like you, Tom. Truth is, I want to be married to you."

"Bad choice because I'm not the marrying kind."

"Then I'll be your woman—live with you anyway."

Zell looked closely at the girl. She was in dead earnest, he saw, and certainly ripe for anything he might have in mind, but he shook his head.

"You better think about this a bit," he said.

"Why? What's there to think about? I've fallen in love with you and I want to be yours—yours only in every way and all the time. If we—"

"Tom!" Reuben Fisk's voice cut in. "Seems like the wind's letting up. You reckon the storm's over?"

Zell did not take his eyes off Purity at the interruption. "Still say you ought to mull this about in your head for a spell," he said, and then turned his attention to the homesteader. "Sure quieting down some. Let's take a look."

Without waiting for Reuben to comply, Tom moved off down the arroyo, pointing for a break in the bank where it would be easier to climb to the level of the prairie above. There was no particular advantage to doing this, for it was possible to gauge the weather equally well from the depths of the wash, but it did furnish him with an excuse to break off the conversation with Purity.

Finding a gap in the wall, Zell made his way to the flat above with Fisk, blowing and puffing, at his heels.

"Settling down for certain," Tom said as the older man halted beside him. "Wind's not so strong and you can see a bit farther."

"About time," Fisk declared. "You suppose we can get started for that river now?"

Zell was staring off to the west. He couldn't be sure, but he thought he'd caught a glimpse of riders—two at least—moving in that direction. He could have been wrong, he knew; at such times on the desert—during a severe sandstorm, extreme heat, or one of the violent cloudbursts that occasionally lashed the country—it was easy to be deceived.

"Let's give it another thirty minutes—"

"Fine. . . . Camp's going to look mighty good tonight. That river you're taking us to, it a fair body of water?"

"Could be dry," Zell replied, and as the homesteader's jaw sagged, added, "but this time of the year there'll likely be water in it. Out here it's something you can never bank on for sure."

Fisk brushed at his jaw, spat. "Big difference in what folks out here call a river and what we do back home," he said, following Tom down the cut in the arroyo bank. "Why, some of them we've seen ain't no more'n ditches."

Zell grinned. "Water's so scarce out here that any creek's a river."

"Expect that's it," Fisk said. "Pity the guv'ment couldn't pipe a lot of the Ohio's floodwater out here to you every spring. We'd all be better off."

"For sure," Tom said, slowing his steps. Purity was standing just where he'd left her—waiting for him to return.

The homesteader, unaware, passed on by his daughter, pausing only long enough to pinch her on the cheek, as he hurried to announce to the others that they would again be underway soon. There was immediate response, and those still clustered at the front of the Tolan wagon began to drift toward their own vehicles.

"Purity, come on!"

It was Patience. She had paused near the Nace wagon, was waiting, arm outstretched.

"I have to go," the girl said, turning away, "but we can meet after supper and talk—make plans."

15

They reached the river not long after sundown, and fording the shallow stream, made camp on its north bank. The men at once saw to the weary teams, leading them to a wider area below the point where they had halted, and there gave each animal a thorough washing down, removing the dust and sand from their coats as well as their eyes, nostrils, and mouths.

"Going to make a big difference in the way they work tomorrow," Caleb Tolan declared, stepping back and surveying the glistening mules and horses, now out of the stream and nibbling at the short grass along its edge.

"I'm only hoping we don't have another windstorm," John Nace said.

"Amen to that!" Fisk added fervently. "One of them in a man's lifetime's plenty enough!"

"Well, it's sure nice now," Tolan remarked, glancing about. "Air's clean and it's warm. Sure never guess what the day's been like if you hadn't gone through it."

Zell, finished with his horse after having turned his hand to assisting Reuben Fisk, was thinking of the two riders he'd seen—or thought he'd seen. He was still not certain, but under the circumstances he felt it best to simply assume he had not been wrong.

And if true, the pair could be members of an out-law gang somewhere in the area. Just as logically they could have been just two men en route north to Prescott or one of the other settlements. There was no way of knowing, of course, and since the whole thing was problematical, Tom decided to make no mention of it—but he would see to it that the usual night precautions were taken.

Lydia Tolan had a fine supper ready—fried meat and potatoes, home-canned green beans, hot biscuits loaded with honey, and strong, black coffee—when Zell, in company Caleb and the somewhat withdrawn George, returned to camp. Everyone was tired, glad the day was done and anxious to find their beds as soon as the meal was over.

The business of setting the night watch came first, however, and when all had finished eating, Zell along with Fisk, Caleb and George Tolan, and John Nace, gathered at the fire to enjoy a last smoke and make the arrangements.

George, declaring himself the least weary of all, volunteered to take the first period of dark to midnight, after which the others could relieve and stand one-hour stints. His shift by choice would be unusually long, he admitted, but he had some serious thinking to do and the lengthy evening would be a good time.

The schedule was agreeable to all, and the matter settled, the meeting broke up. Zell, after extending his thanks to Lydia for a fine supper, headed for the spot near the stream where he'd dropped his gear.

He felt much better after the meal, and the impulse to go down stream a distance, strip off, and have a bath came over him. Washing off the horses had helped some, but he still felt gritty, and the idea became more appealing as he crossed through the camp, pausing only long enough at the Nace wagon to bid Abby, cleaning up her supper dishes, a good night.

Purity was waiting for him when he reached his gear. She was sitting on the blanket roll, legs extended in front of her, hands clasped in her lap, and with hair pulled back into a bun on her neck, she looked not only very fetching but considerably older.

"Are you surprised to find me here?" she asked as Tom halted and considered her with a frown. "I said we'd talk more about us after supper. . . . I got Patience to do my chores for me."

Zell moved in closer, and pulling off his hat, dropped to his heels near his saddle. Unbuckling one of the saddlebags, he took out the bottle of whiskey and helped himself to a good drink. That done, he restored the liquor to its place and struck a match to a fresh cigar. Off in the thin brush that lined the stream insects had begun to clack noisily.

"Not sure what we've got to talk about," he said after a time. She was a real pretty girl, well-built, and though young, she was old enough to marry; he reckoned that qualified her as being grown.

"Us—that's what. Have you forgotten already the things we said?"

"You said," he corrected gently. "This is all your idea."

What Purity had in mind was clear, and ordinarily Tom Zell would have welcomed her, but for some incomprehensible reason he was holding back. What the hell was wrong with him, he wondered, staring off into the star- and moon-lit night. Never in his adult life had he backed off from taking a woman—any woman, free or belonging to another man, be he friend or otherwise—but here he was now refusing a desirable young girl who was literally throwing herself at him. Why?

Tom could find no satisfactory answer to the puzzling question, and getting to his feet, stepped up to Purity and extended a hand to assit her in rising.

"Expect your folks are looking for you about now. Not right to let them worry."

Her lips tightened as she studied him. "You mean that you—I—"

"I mean we're both plenty tired after a day like we've been through, and needing rest. I aim to go downstream a piece, take a swim, and wash off if I can find water deep enough—and then turn in."

"But, Tom, I thought we—"

"Tomorrow's another day. Let's see how we feel about things then."

Anger flashed in Purity Fisk's dark eyes. Jerking free of him, she drew up stiffly. "All right, if that's how you want it," she said curtly. "And far as I'm concerned, there's no need for us to talk tomorrow."

Wheeling abruptly, the girl hurried off into the deepening shadows, head high and shoulders a square, outraged line.

Zell waited until she had disappeared beyond the Nace wagon, and then restoring his hat to its place on his head, walked to the edge of the river and started downstream. The night would soon be complete, the stars and moon shedding soft light over the land; and with the air warm and still, with no hint of the surging wind that had scourged the hills and flats earlier, he was looking forward to a pleasant and relaxing time in the water.

A short distance below where they had taken care of the horses, Tom halted. The stream made a sharp bend at that point and a pool, not large enough to swim in but one fairly deep, had been formed. Finding a place on the bank near a stand of Apache plume where prairie grass was growing, he removed his clothing, taking care to hang his gunbelt on a stout limb of a shrub, where it would be within quick and easy reach.

The water was cool, and the moment he entered and sank to his knees in order for it to flow over his body, he felt better.

"You mind if I join you?"

At the sound of the familiar voice, Tom twisted about. Abby was standing on the bank where he had discarded his clothing; she was looking down at him, a blanket about her shoulders.

"I feel so dusty—"

Zell grinned. "Come on in—there's plenty of room in the tub."

Purity stopped at the end of the family wagon, placed her hands on the tailgate, and hung there stunned, disappointed, and deeply hurt. She had offered herself to Tom Zell and he had brushed her off with the weak excuse that he was tired—too tired—and that they could talk about it tomorrow. And then, worst of all, she'd reacted like a child, getting angry and flouncing off.

"Purity, you'd better hurry and get in bed," Patience's low voice came to her from beneath the wagon. "The folks haven't missed you yet, but—"

"I'm not sleepy," the younger girl said tartly.

"You better come to bed anyway. Just where have you been, as if I couldn't guess?"

"That's my business—"

"It's going to be everybody's business if you aren't careful," Patience declared reprovingly. "I saw

George watching you when you were with Zell, and it was plain he didn't like it—fussing over him the way you were."

"Who cares what George Tolan likes?" Purity snapped, and then coming to a decision, she turned away. "I'll be back shortly. There's something I've got to do."

"What if Mama asks—" Patience began, her voice rising.

"You'll think of something," Purity replied, and hurried on.

She'd find Tom and make amends, apologize for getting angry and acting like a ninny. He said he was going for a swim, but maybe he hadn't gone yet; maybe he was still there by the creek where he'd put his blankets and saddle.

But Zell was nowhere in sight. Standing in the darkness, Purity gave the problem thought. He'd mentioned he intended to find a place downstream, one deep enough for swimming; that's where she'd find him, somewhere below camp.

Wading across the shallow stream to the opposite bank, where she would not be seen by anyone in the camp who might still be up and about, Purity moved off. Pausing every few feet, stepping in close to the quietly flowing water, and looking beyond the brush that grew along the bank, she searched for Tom.

She heard his voice before locating him. It was low, almost as if he were talking to himself—which he probably was, since he would be there alone. Moving in closer, Purity pushed aside the scraggly growth that blocked her view and looked toward the source of the sound. As if struck across the face, she recoiled instantly.

Tom and Abby Nace were sitting on a blanket at

the edge of the stream. Neither had any clothing on, apparently having been in swimming or bathing together—and it was not hard to guess what else.

It was clear now. He had sent her back to the wagon, pleading weariness, while all the time he had it in mind to meet Abby. They had probably fixed it up between themselves some time during the evening or possibly earlier.

Purity bit at her lower lip, brushed at the tears beginning to seep from her eyes. Tom Zell wanted Abby more than he did her—that, too, was clear. But she wasn't going to give him up. She had one big thing in her favor besides being young: she was unmarried, while Abby Nace was another man's wife. She'd make a point of that tomorrow when they talked—if there was to be a tomorrow for them. She wasn't sure she could forgive Tom—or even wanted to.

Wheeling, fighting tears, Purity started back up the short slope leading from the stream to the flat above, stumbling a bit in her haste. Why did this have to happen to her? Why couldn't Tom—

A dark shape rose suddenly out of the brush to her left. A strong arm went about her, clamped her in a viselike grip, a hand pressed tight against her lips as a second figure emerged from the ragged growth on her right.

"*Ai-eee, mama!*" an accented voice said hoarsely. "Look what I have caught, *compadre*—a tender young dove!"

"Just right for plucking," the second man, smelling strongly of sweat and tobacco like the first, agreed. "We have a prize!"

"It is I with the prize, my friend—it is not for you to make such claim."

Purity, over her initial shock, fear now racing through her like fire in late-summer grass, began to struggle fiercely, twisting and turning as she endeavored to break free. But the arm that encircled did not relent and one of the dark shadows laughed softly.

"She sure is a squirmer—"

In that moment Purity managed to dislodge the fingers crushing her lips, and taking a deep breath, she put everything she had into a frantic cry.

"Help! Help me!"

16

Zell lunged to his feet at Purity's cry of terror—the recollection of the two riders he'd seen earlier now a reality in his mind.

"What—what do you think's wrong?" Abby asked, also rising and putting on her gown.

"Hard to say, but I've got a hunch," Tom replied, hurriedly picking up the blanket that had been spread on the ground and thrusting it into her hands. Pulling on his pants and stamping into his boots, he added, "Head back to your wagon—and stay in the brush. Nobody'll see you."

Abby shook her head. "That doesn't matter. What about you—your clothes?"

"Went swimming—that's all the explanation I'll need," he said, jerking his gun belt off the brush from which it hung. There were sounds of urgent activity back at the camp—voices shouting questions, the thud of running feet. Purity's scream had aroused the others.

"Hurry," Zell continued, pushing Abby toward the brush bordering the stream, and then pistol in hand, belt slung across a bare shoulder, he splashed through the water to the opposite side of the river and headed for the point from which the girl's cry seemed to have come.

He wondered what had happened, what she was doing there in the night—and then, abruptly, it came to him. Purity had followed him! He had said he was going for a swim. She had changed her mind about returning to the Fisk wagon and set out to find him, and during her course along the stream had encountered someone—outlaws, most likely the two he had seen, or it could be Indians. Regardless which, it didn't matter. He must reach the girl, help her. When it came right down to bedrock, he was responsible for her being there.

Reaching the far side of the stream, Zell rushed up the bank to the level flat above. A thought came to him: had Purity seen him and Abby? In a way he hoped so, for it would make it clear to the girl where she stood with him. It would be cruel, no doubt, but he had to make her see that she would be making a mistake—that she should marry—

Tom whirled, pistol ready, at the crashing of brush to his left. An instant later George Tolan burst into view, rifle in hand.

"Where—" he began, and then caught his words when he saw Zell, only partly dressed, awaiting him.

"Ahead—I figure," Tom said, answering the unfinished question. "Was downstream taking a swim—heard her yell. Let's go."

The relief that flooded young Tolan's face was evident as he and Zell hurried on. Noises back along the bank of the river told them the other men had arrived from camp to take a hand in the matter.

"What do you figure happened?" George asked, reaching deep for breath as they pressed on, searching the shadow-filled brush for signs of the girl.

"Must've gone for a walk, run into somebody—"

"Somebody?"

"Outlaws—or could be Indians."

"Lord!" George Tolan muttered in a horrified voice. "I hope not! If I—"

"Look out!" Zell shouted, and threw himself to the ground as two horses, their riders bent low, suddenly broke into the open and raced toward a clump of mesquite a dozen yards away.

The man in the lead twisted about, fired point-blank at George, but the bullet went wide. Zell heard Tolan make an answering shot as, prone, he leveled his own weapon at the second rider. He was the one of importance. Astride the rear of his saddle, he had Purity in front of him, one arm encircling her waist while he held the reins in the hand of the other.

Careful, patient, Tom waited until the man with his struggling prisoner was directly opposite, and then, when the chance of hitting the girl was at its smallest, he triggered his pistol.

The rider yelled, rocked back, arms flung wide. The horse, lines suddenly going slack, slowed, veered, and as the rider fell from his back, came to a trembling halt.

Zell came to his feet, but George Tolan was ahead of him, reaching Purity's side well ahead of him. The gunshots had directed the other men to the spot, and they, too, were hurrying up.

Tom, leaving it all to George, now lifting the girl off the saddle, hurried on, hoping to get a shot at the second rider. He reached the mesquite, stopped. There was no one in sight, although the desert, bathed in strong, silver light, was clearly visible for a considerable distance.

Zell swore deeply, turned, and headed back for the

others. If the pair who had encountered Purity were part of an outlaw gang, which was very likely, the one who had escaped would carry back word of the wagon train camped along the Santa Maria, and plans to raid it would be made.

Tom shook his head, spat. Luck was running against him. First the busters, then the sandstorm, and now outlaws—Mexicans, or at least the one he'd dropped appeared to be dressed in the fashion of the *bandidos* from below the border. The one who had escaped could have been an American, but he couldn't be certain.

"That bastard get away?"

It was Caleb Tolan hurrying to meet him. On beyond the homesteader, the remaining members of the party—including Abby—had gathered around Purity and George.

Zell said, "Was gone by the time I got to open ground. Purity all right?"

Fisk, glancing about as Tom and Tolan approached, and overhearing, said, "Scared a-plenty, but nothing more. I reckon this'll cure her of wandering around at nights."

"Lucky for her you was close by," Tolan said. "George said you'd gone for a swim. Can see you didn't have time to grab up all your duds."

"We're mighty grateful to you," Martha Fisk said, coming into the conversation. "I hate to think what would've become of our girl if those men had gotten away with her."

Zell shrugged, smiled, and casting a covert glance at Abby, standing behind the elderly woman, crossed to where the outlaw lay. Rolling the man to his back, he knelt, studied the dark features all but concealed by beard and mustache. He had been right: the man was Mexican.

"Know him?" Fisk asked.

Tom drew himself upright, turned. The three homesteaders had followed him. "Stranger to me. He's a Mex."

"You think there'll be more of them hanging around—a gang, I mean?"

There was no point in deceiving them. Far better they be aware of the danger they now faced.

"Good chance there is. Usually run in a bunch."

"How many would you say there'll be?"

"No telling. Ten, twelve, maybe more. They like to stick together, so's there'll always be enough of them to raid even the big wagon trains."

"I'm beginning to think we'd have been better off on the main road," John Nace said. "At least we maybe'd had some company."

Tom stirred indifferently. "I figured the chances of us having no trouble on this route would be good, but there's never any guarantees."

"Of course there ain't," Tolan agreed. "You couldn't expect to know for sure where them gangs of cutthroats are hanging out—or ain't."

"Not when they're running wild all over the country," Fisk added.

Nace was unconvinced. "Seems to me it would be his business to know—or least have a good idea—"

"Forget it, John," Caleb Tolan cut in, impatient at the man's unreasonableness. "I'm just more than thankful we hired him. Now, let's get back to the wagons and catch some sleep. Ain't going to be long till daylight, and we could be in for a bad day, ain't that right, Tom?"

Zell nodded, and turning, started back down to the stream as the others began to move toward the camp.

"Ain't you coming?" Tolan called after him.

Zell waved them on. "Got to collect the rest of my clothes—I'll be along. . . . Good night."

17

Martha Fisk insisted they take time to bury the dead outlaw that next morning, stating firmly that it was the Christian thing to do, and thus they were almost an hour getting underway.

"What about his horse?" Tolan had wanted to know. "He ain't much, but it'd be wrong to just let him run loose. Expect there's wolves around here."

"Claim him if you're of a mind," Zell said. "No brand on him. Makes him anybody's property."

"Think I'll just do that," the pilgrim said, and had then added the lean, little black to the spare team of mules trailing his wagon.

They had moved out shortly after that—John Nace and Abby in the lead, the Fisks occupying the center space in the train, leaving the Tolans to bring up the rear. The sun was already hot and there was no reminder of the previous day's windstorm, but a slight breeze had come drifting with first light that made traveling pleasant.

Zell, following his custom of riding out in front of the train, occasionally circling wide to either side and dropping back to the rear periodically as he kept an eye out for trouble, saw nothing of Abby. John Nace sat on the seat of his wagon alone—glum, hard-cornered face kept straight ahead as always. Abby, Tom supposed, was finding things to do inside the vehicle.

He had seen little of Purity Fisk, also. She had avoided him during the early-morning meal and subsequently when preparations to pull out were being made, and thus he had become more convinced the girl had come upon him and Abby while they were enjoying themselves by the stream.

He regretted that it had happened in just that manner, but as he'd thought earlier, it would have a beneficial effect. And it seemed it did, Purity was again showing an interest in George Tolan, and that was all to the good and just as it should be.

He was pointing now for the peaked mountains looming up gray-blue to the west—called the Rawhides by some, the Artillerys by others. It was a goal the train would reach by sundown if all went well, but Zell, curiously ill at ease, was reluctant to plan on it.

The more he thought about it, the more certain he became that the two outlaws were members of a gang and they, having spotted the homesteaders' camp, had closed in to size up possibilities. Once they had seen the strength of the train and reckoned its value, the idea was to return to their own camp and report.

Evidently they were in the process of doing just that when they stumbled onto Purity Fisk. Unable to resist such a prize, they had attempted to take her with them, but the kidnapping had failed and one of the two had died for his efforts. His partner, however had escaped, and it would be he who carried the word to the rest of the outlaws.

But there had been no sign of riders so far in any direction as the wagons rolled steadily across the desert for the distant hills, and by noon, when a halt was called alongside a small cluster of cottonwoods growing in an arroyo, Zell was beginning to think there perhaps was no large gang of outlaws after all, that the pair they had encountered were nothing more than that—two renegades in search of easy pickings.

Reuben Fisk voiced that thought, also, as they rested in the shade and ate a sparing lunch of dried meat, bread, and coffee.

"I'm wondering if them two just didn't happen along," he said.

"I'm hoping that was it," Zell replied, his glance on Abby off to one side with Lydia Tolan. She looked fresh and alive, her eyes had a sparkle to them and her skin had taken on a warm glow. "But we're not out of the woods yet—not till we get to the Colorado."

"Was just thinking," Caleb Tolan said, drawing out his blackened briar pipe and tamping shreds of tobacco into its bowl, "we've got a saddle horse now and there ain't no sense in George just setting there on the wagon seat by me when he could be riding with you, helping keep an eye out for trouble and the like—that is, if you're willing."

"Be jake with me," Tom replied. "Can use some help—and the company."

Caleb smiled broadly. "It'll sure please the boy," he said, turning, called to his son, who was standing with Purity a short distance away. "George, come here a minute."

Young Tolan, with Purity at his side, crossed over at once and halted in front of the men. "Yeh, Pa?"

"Had a talk with Tom. Said he'd be right pleased to have you riding with him."

George Tolan's face lit up. "That's sure fine! I been hoping I could do more'n just spell you driving," he said, and turned to Zell. "Reckon I ought to thank you."

"No thanks necessary," Tom replied. Evidently the

hostility he'd seen in George earlier, when Purity had insisted on centering her attention on him, had passed. "Can use your help."

At that moment the girl raised her eyes, settled them on Zell. He read accusation in them—and a measure of relief as well.

"I think I need to thank you, too," she said.

"No need. Just pleased that I was handy when you yelled."

"Yes, and I was lucky that George was such a good shot. If he'd missed that outlaw he would've hit me—and he could have missed altogether, too. Then I—"

Zell had swung glance to George Tolan. The younger man was looking off across the desert, now shimmering in the midday sun. At the girl's words he turned his eyes to Tom, met his gaze squarely. There was a plea in them—a plea for understanding.

Zell shrugged. That George had taken credit for bringing down Purity's would-be kidnapper meant nothing to him; and if the lie would—as it evidently had—bring the pair closer together, it was all right with him.

"Was good shooting for sure," he said, coming to his feet and giving the signal to move out.

It was late in the afternoon when he spotted a band of riders well to the north. George Tolan, astride the dead outlaw's horse, caught sight of the party at about the same moment and hurriedly called the matter to Tom's attention.

"Outlaws—or maybe Indians—that what you figure?"

"Hard to tell from here," Zell replied, studying the country through which the train was presently passing. They were in the open and there was no doubt the wagons had been seen by the riders.

"Looks like they're a-heading this way," George said. "You reckon it's the gang them two last night belonged to?"

"Probably," Tom said.

A mile on ahead there appeared to be an area where the earth, in aeons past, had erupted and formed a solitary mass of rock. Through the centuries growth had taken hold and now the dark ragged surface was covered with weeds and brush. Smaller, similar mounds lay to the south.

"Drop back and tell your pa and the others to head for that big pile of rocks," Zell directed, pointing to the formation. "Expect they've spotted those riders, too, but you best call their attention to them."

"Could be they're friendly people—not outlaws."

"There's a chance," Tom admitted, "but I'll lay odds they're renegades. Tell your pa and them to whip up their teams. We want to get to those rocks in a hurry where we can hole up till we know what we're up against."

"They're coming pretty fast. You think we can make it—"

"Can if you'll get back there and pass the word," Zell said, impatient. "I'll ride ahead, pick a place for the wagons to pull into."

"Going right now," George said, "but first I want to tell you something. Back there, when we were nooning and Purity talked about me shooting that outlaw, I—I'm obliged to you for not setting her—and the others—straight. I know it was wrong, but it just sort of got started and—"

"Forget it," Tom said with a wave of his hand. "You maybe'll just get the chance to really show how good you are at shooting."

18

The wagons made it to the formation with only minutes to spare. Zell, there well ahead of them, had scouted the rock and brush-studded mound until he'd located a fairly deep bay, one large enough to admit the wagons and afford protection on all but the front side.

He had just treated himself to a drink when Nace arrived in the lead wagon; the others followed closely. Directing the homesteaders to pull as far into the cove as possible, Zell then dismounted, and taking his rifle, hurried to the entrance of the shallow canyon.

The riders had at first quickened their pace, but when it became apparent to them that they would be unable to intercept the train before it reached the safety of the rocks, they slowed and were now approaching at an easy lope.

Brushing aside the sweat gathered on his forehead and misting his eyes, Tom Zell squinted at the riders. There were an even dozen of them, and the man in the lead, on a coal-black horse with white stockings, looked familiar even at a distance.

A rattling of gravel and dry leaves behind him drew Tom around. Fisk and Nace, with both Tolans, had joined him.

"They still coming?" George asked, out of breath from hurrying.

Zell said, "Still coming—a round dozen of them."

"You figure they're outlaws?" Fisk asked.

"Pretty certain. You wouldn't find a bunch of decent men hanging about here. Folks cross the desert fast as they can."

"They're a long way from where you said they'd probably be," Nace observed, studying the riders. "There wasn't supposed to be any outlaws here."

"Oh, for hell's sake, John," Fisk exploded before Zell could make a comment. "Tom's done explained that to you. We can't expect him to keep tabs on all the outlaws in the country!"

"For sure," Caleb Tolan said, agreeing. "I bet there's some special reason for them being this far off the main road. That right, Tom?"

Zell, his attention riveted to the riders, was paying little mind to what was being said. He frowned, nodded to the elder Tolan.

"Missed what you asked—"

The homesteader repeated his supposition. Zell's shoulders stirred. "Could be a half a dozen reasons, but I expect this bunch has been hanging around Prescott—on north and west of here. Been a lot of traveling in and out of there lately . . . Joe Durango," he added in a whisper.

"What's that?" Fisk asked.

"Just recognized the leader of that gang—jasper on the black horse. Name's Joe Durango."

"He is bad one?"

"One of the worst. Half-breed—Mex and Apache Indian. Does a lot of dealing with the comancheros."

"Comancheros?" Caleb Tolan echoed. "Who or what are they?"

"Mexicans, usually. Trade with the Apaches and the Comanches—buy the stuff the Indians steal or get when they raid some wagon train or ranch, then sell it in the towns below the border. Includes women—men, too."

"Can understand what they'd want the women for, but men—"

"Lot of mining down in Mexico and there's always a demand for men to work the mines. Amounts to slave labor, and a miner's life is plenty short."

Zell glanced down over his shoulder to the wagons and located Abby. She was with the other women, standing in the narrow shade being cast by one of the vehicles. All were well out of the line of fire if shooting developed. Satisfied as to that, he came back around again fell to studying the outlaws. They were near enough now to see distinctly.

"Some of them look like Indians," Fisk said. "Wearing them white drawers and no shirt—and a rag around their head."

"That's what they are. Could be Apaches or maybe Comanches, but most of the bunch are Mexicans. Only a couple of white men there, I'd say, but they're all tough customers to go up against."

"You going to let them come close and then start shooting—that what you're aiming to do?" Nace wanted to know.

Zell shook his head. "That saguaro there—the one that looks like a big candleholder—it'll be the deadline. And we let them talk first. The shooting, if it comes down to it, will be later. With twelve of them to five of us, I'd like to try talking them into thinking we're too small to bother with."

As if reading Zell's mind, Durango and his men

rode up to where they were more or less abreast the big cactus and halted.

"Friends," the outlaw leader called out, raising his hand in the sign of peace. "We are friends!"

Zell, making a show of it, leveled his rifle at the man. "Don't say friend to me, Durango! I know what you are!"

"You know me, eh?" the outlaw replied, obviously pleased. "You are known to me?"

"No, but I'm warning you to keep moving. We don't have anything you want—unless it's trouble."

"Trouble? Do not try to fool me, *amigo*. I watch you through the glasses. You are but five men and we are many more."

"Five good shooters," Zell said. "Forted up like we are, we can even the odds mighty fast. Best you ride on, leave us be or you'll lose more of your men."

"Ah, yes, poor Ortega. He had a great hunger for a woman. It was the death of him. . . . Good friend, can you spare us a small amount of water? We have been many days without—"

"You're a liar, Durango. There's water in the Santa Maria, and you damn well know it!"

The outlaw leader's shoulders lifted, fell in a gesture of resignation. Lifting a hand, he brushed the high-peaked-crown Mexican hat he was wearing to the back of his head. The skin of his face in the direct sunlight shone darkly.

"Are we going to open up on them?" George Tolan asked in a taut voice.

"Not unless they make a run at us," Zell answered. "They're out of range, anyway."

"It is sad," the half-breed called in a regretful tone. "We would be your friends, but you have refuse us. Now it will be necessary to—"

The bluff had failed. Tom sighed down the barrel of his rifle at Durango. The distance was too great for accurate shooting, as he'd told young Tolan, but he just might get lucky. Aiming high, he triggered a shot.

The bullet spurted sand a few yards in front of the outlaw. It was a useless attempt, but it did have its salutary effect; Durango realized the pilgrims were ready and waiting, and holed up as they were in the rocks, he and his men would pay a high price if a head-on charge was attempted.

As the echoes of the solitary rifle shot rolled out across the desert, the outlaws remained unmoving, having a discussion of some sort, and then with no further sign or comment, all wheeled about and rode slowly off toward the south.

"They're backing off—leaving," Caleb said with a deep sigh of relief. "Thank the Lord for—"

"Can't see Durango passing up a plum like us," Zell cut in. "He's giving up too quick."

"He ain't," Fisk said a moment later as the outlaws, reaching one of the other mounds of weeds and rocks, halted and began to dismount. "Looks like they're going to bed down right there."

"What do you reckon they aim to do now?" Tolan wondered.

"Hold off—wait for dark, then come at us," Zell said. "Be a cinch then."

Nace forearmed sweat from his face. "That's for sure. We won't stand a chance if they move in on us from a half a dozen different points."

"Expect we can hold some of them off even then," Fisk said, glancing about, "if we get up in them rocks, but there's bound to be a few slip by and get behind us. What do you think, Tom? Looks to me like we've got ourselves in between a rock and a hard place."

"Maybe—but we can play the same game."

"Meaning what?"

"We'll wait for night, then hit them."

Reuben Fisk hawked, spat. "Five of us against twelve of them?"

"Won't need us all. I figure three—me and a couple of you—would stand the best chance of slipping up on them and getting the job done. Five would be risky—too big a chance of somebody making a noise and tipping them off."

"Count me in," George said at once.

Zell had already made his selections. George was more or less untested, young, and he had a life with Purity before him; he would not be one. The same applied to John Nace, but for a different reason. Should the man get himself killed, Abby might think he had arranged for her husband to die, and if there was to be a future together for them, even though the Naces as a married couple appeared to have reached a parting of the ways, the disturbing thought would always be there in her mind standing between them like a dark shadow.

And there were others in the wagon train who would entertain like beliefs. He had not missed the meaningful glances exchanged by Martha Fisk and Lydia Tolan when they saw Abby and him together. And there was Purity: she knew far better than any of them the nature of his relationship with John Nace's wife, and doubtless would not hesitate to reveal it if the time came—and the wagging tongues such would evoke were something he'd not permit Abby to be subjected to.

Tom Zell frowned, scrubbed at his jaw as he continued to stare at the outlaws, now prowling about in the rocks and brush of the distant mound as they sought protection from the sun. Unconsciously he had included Abby Nace in his plans and thoughts. It was another new experience; first his refusal of Purity Fisk, and now his deep concern and consideration for Abby. He, who had always looked upon all women as fair game to be enjoyed and then forgotten within the space of a few hours, now found himself thinking seriously of a future with one! What had come over him?

"Can figure on me," Fisk stated.

The words brought Zell from his deep reflections. "Had you and Caleb in mind," he said. "Figured it would be better for George and Nace to stay at the wagons and see to it that the women are protected in case a couple of Durango's bunch get by us."

George started to protest, but the older Tolan hushed him with a wave of his hand. "No, Zell's right. You look after your ma. If anything happens to me, you'll be around to see she's taken care of. Same goes for Purity and the others. Don't want any of them falling into the hands of—"

"I'll be there, too," Nace said stiffly.

"I know that, John," Tolan replied. "Was just making it plain to George that he'd be responsible."

"It all set then?" Zell asked. And when they each nodded agreement, he added, "As well get back to camp then and rest up. Durango and his bunch won't try anything till it's dark, maybe not even till he thinks we're asleep. Whichever—it's important we make our move before they do."

19

"Keep a low fire going," Zell said as the members of the wagon train gathered around him. It was full dark and the time to move out had come. "Don't want it too light—just enough to make Durango and his crowd think we're still here. George, you got those stakes ready"

"Fixed three, like you said," the younger Tolan answered. "Got the hats and coats to hang on them, too."

"Soon as we're gone, stick them in the ground between the fire and them so's it'll look like men sitting around waiting, taking it easy. Idea's to make that bunch think we're all here in camp. If we can do that, your pa, Fisk, and I'll be able to sneak up on them without any trouble." Tom paused, glanced about. "Any questions"

Martha Fisk laid a hand on her husband's arm. "I don't like Reuben taking such a big chance. Those men—outlaws—they've lived with a gun and know how to use it. All Reuben's ever done is hunt—"

"Now don't you go getting cold feet, Ma," Fisk said hurriedly. "You know dang well I can take care of myself—have for a lot of years, and I sure ain't no greenhorn with this rifle. Besides, we know there'd come times like this."

114

"We all did," Caleb Tolan said. "Told ourselves it was the chance we'd have to take if we wanted to start a new life some place where things wasn't civilized. My wife's remembering that."

Martha Tolan smiled wanly, reached out, took Caleb's hand into her own. "I am, but don't you go doing something foolish—like trying to be a hero."

Caleb grinned. "I ain't that ambitious," he said.

Zell continued to look around. He got no further response. "I'll meet you men on the south side—over there by the stand of mesquite, in fifteen minutes," he said then, nodding to Fisk and Tolan. "Keep out of sight getting there. Don't want them to guess what we're up to."

Pivoting, Tom doubled back to where he'd laid his gear. There was nothing he had forgotten; he simply wanted to have one last drink from his bottle, he assured himself, but there was a vague hope present in his mind that Abby would manage to come and wish him luck.

He was still surprised at himself and the change that had overtaken him. A man who never in his life had considered any woman seriously had suddenly become aware that one now occupied his thoughts completely. It was a puzzle to him as to how it had come about.

Taking the bottle from its corner in his saddlebags, Zell tipped it to his lips and had a deep swallow. Replacing the cork, he knelt, returned the liquor to the leather pouch.

"Tom—"

At the sound of Abby's voice Zell came to his feet and wheeled. She was standing at the edge of the darkness alongside a clump of brush, barely visible in the still-weak moon- and starlight.

"I had to come—beg you to be careful—"

Zell flung a quick glance toward the fire placed in the center of the camp. The women had gathered next to one of the wagons. Nace and George Tolan were engaged in erecting the stakes upon which clothing would be placed to create the illusion of men hunched before the flames.

"Was wondering—hoping—I'd see you," he said, crossing to her.

Abby met him with open arms, and for a long minute they stood locked in embrace with no need for words to express thoughts or feelings. And then Zell abruptly pulled away.

"I'll be back," he murmured.

"I'll pray that you will," Abby said as he moved off.

Circling the wagons, Tom hurried past the two men and the women unseen and joined Caleb Tolan and Reuben Fisk waiting for him at the entrance to the cove.

"Getting lighter," Fisk said. "Sure ain't going to be no picnic sneaking up on that bunch."

Zell studied the distant mound of rocks where the outlaws were camped. There were two or three small fires visible and occasionally an indistinct figure appeared in the flare. It was not possible to determine at that distance if any of the men were sleeping or not—or even if all twelve of them were still there. Tom turned his attention hopefully to the sky. There were a few clouds in evidence but none that would do them any good.

"It's not going to get any darker," he said then. "Let's get started. We'll keep close to the rocks till we come to the end of these along here. Can swing wide from there, work our way up to their camp from behind."

"Still going to be plenty of open ground to cover," Tolan said doubtfully.

"Stay low and use the bushes. Long as a man does that, it's hard to spot him at night—even in the open."

Zell glanced at the men, nodded. "Luck," he said, and moved off.

Tolan and Fisk immediately stepped in behind him, and at a crouch they hurried along the foot of the ragged formation, keeping close to the rocks and brush until they reached the point where it began to curve back toward the west.

"That was easy," Tolan said, looking to the outlaw camp, now well above them. "Now'll come the hard part."

"We'll make it," Zell said. "Just follow me and stay close."

"Sort of like going duck hunting—sneaking up on a flock in the dark," Tolan remarked.

"Ducks can't shoot back, Fisk said dryly.

Tom grinned at the comment, and pressed on. He was moving fast but careful, taking a course that hopscotched from one brush clump or low sink to another. They gained one of the smaller mounds, paused behind it. All three of them were breathing hard, and the warmness of the night had brought sweat beads to their foreheads and dampened their clothing.

"Can get in back of them from there," Zell said, pointing to another rock and brush-covered pile a hundred yards or so to the north of them. "We've got it made once we reach that."

Tolan nodded his understanding. Fisk said, "Been keeping an eye on them. Ain't none of them left their camp yet and headed for ours."

"Durango's in no rush," Zell said. "Figures he's got us pinned down and outnumbered. He won't do anything till he's good and ready. . . . Let's go."

Low, Tom moved out from behind their ragged screen of stunted growth and ran for the next mound, Fisk and Tolan close on his heels. Again breathless, they reached it. They were now near enough to smell the smoke from the renegades' fires and hear the sound of their voices. One among them was singing in a high off-key tone, while bursts of laughter exploded from others now and then.

"I ain't never killed a man," Reuben Fisk said haltingly.

"Me neither," Tolan added. "I ain't so sure I—"

Zell looked closely at the two men. Light from overhead was now beaming down upon the desert full strength, and the grim lines in the faces of the homesteaders and the uncertainty in their eyes were evident. He shook his head.

"Like to say you could back off now, that I'd take care of this for you, but I can't. Odds would be too high, twelve to one. Best way is to not think about it, then when the times comes you'll just react and start doing what you know you have to."

"Hope I'll react—like you say," Reuben said uncertainly.

"You just think about what it'll be like for your wife and daughters if that bunch gets their hands on them," Tom said, and let it hang there to have its effect on the homesteader. Then, after a few moments, "Ready?"

"Just say the word," Fisk replied, his voice now firm and determined.

"We'll slip up from behind, like I've said. When we're set, I'll give the signal to close in and start shooting. Surprise will be with us, but watch your step from here on. Crack a dry branch or stumble, and the noise'll sure give us away."

Tom waited no longer, and again hunched low, rifle ready, quickly crossed the fifty-yard strip of open desert lying behind the mound where the outlaws had halted. The singer had abandoned his plaintive efforts, but the sound of voices was much clearer. Zell could not see the men in the camp from where he and the homesteaders had stopped, and motioning to them to remain where they were, he dropped to the still-warm ground, and flat on his belly, wormed his way to where he would have a view. Reaching that point, he raised his head carefully and made a count.

Twelve men—all lolling about the fires. Some were drinking from a bottle being passed around, others were chewing on jerky or smoking limp cigarettes— but all at ease awaiting the moment when their *jefe*, Joe Durango, would give the word to raid the *gringo* wagon train.

Zell shifted his attention to the camp of the homesteaders. The fire there burned as he'd directed—small, but large enough to silhouette three figures hunkered before it, as well as two others who trod restlessly back and forth as if on sentry duty.

Everything was as it should be: the outlaws were still holding off and all was well at the wagon train. Carefully backing away from the edge of the renegades' camp, Zell wheeled and returned to Fisk and Tolan and advised them of such.

"Doubt if Durango will hold off much longer," he said, and cautioning the two men to use care, began again to make his way toward the front of the mound—this time with rifle ready to fire.

Fisk and Tolan, taking their cue from him, followed closely. Near the front of the formation and with the outlaws now in clear view, Zell motioned to the homesteaders to separate, spread out to more or less form a line. Then, with them in position, he again started forward. A half a dozen slow, quiet steps, and he paused once more. The outlaws were still sprawled about in the flare of their fires and were so near that the reflection of the flickering flames was mirrored in their eyes.

Tom nodded to the homesteaders and pointed to a low clump of brush a short distance ahead, indicating that when they reached it, the moment to open fire would be at hand. Tolan and Fisk signified their understanding, and all started forward again.

A sudden rattling in the brush ahead of them brought Tom and the homesteaders to an abrupt halt. A dark shape bolted from the shadows in which it had been hiding and raced off into the night. Zell swore silently. A small desert fox was startled into flight by his appearance.

The damage was done—and there was nothing to do about it. Several of the outlaws, hearing the fox in its hurried escape, turned to look. At the sight of three men standing just beyond the reach of their fire's glow, they yelled a warning and sprang erect.

"Now!" Zell shouted, and aiming his rifle into the confusion of abruptly scrambling outlaws, began to fire as rapidly as he could work the lever and press the trigger of the weapon.

Nearby he heard the roar of Caleb Tolan's old ten-gauge shotgun and the crack of Fisk's rifle. Three of the renegades were down, he saw, and the others were running for their horses, barely visible through the swirling powder smoke. Suddenly bullets began to whip by him as the outlaws, over their initial surprise, began a return fire.

"Down!" he shouted, and dropped full length to the sand.

His rifle clicked on an empty chamber. Letting the gun fall, he drew his pistol, snapped a shot at one of the renegades attempting to mount a shying horse just beyond the mound. The man threw up his arms and fell as the bullet found its mark.

A dark shadow hovered over him suddenly. Zell rolled, brought up his weapon to fire, checked himself. It was Caleb Tolan, bent forward and advancing toward the fleeing outlaws.

"Get down," Zell shouted, reaching for the homesteader.

Tolan paused, and as if only then aware of what he was doing, started to heed Tom's urgent yell. In that same moment he staggered, sank to the ground as a bullet drove into him. Cursing, he tried to rise. Zell pulled himself to his knees, grabbed the older man by the arm, and pulled him back down.

As he settled back, he felt a stinging shock in his left arm just above the elbow, realized he, too, had been hit. Ignoring the pain and satisfied now that Caleb Tolan would remain where he lay, Zell resumed firing at the dark figures milling about in the area where the outlaws had picketed their horses. Fisk—it came to him suddenly—was no longer using his weapon and Tom had a quick fear that the man, like Tolan, had also been hit. Regret flooded through him: he shouldn't have let them take part in the shoot-out; he should have known they weren't equal to it. And then a sign of relief slipped from his tightly set lips as he heard the pilgrim sing out.

"They're running! They're pulling out!"

Zell drew himself to his knees and had his look. The homesteader was right. Durango, with what remained of his gang, was riding off into the desert.

"How many'd we get?'"

There was a note of triumph in Fisk's tone. Tom, reloading, got to his feet. Nearby, Caleb Tolan was also rising, which brought a smile of relief to Zell. Caleb was still alive—hurt, but not dead as he'd feared. Favoring his wounded arm, he walked slowly into the center of the camp, glancing about as he did.

"Looks like five of them," he said, answering Fisk's question. "How's it with you?"

"I'm doing fine," the homesteader replied as he halted beside Tolan. "Caleb's took a bullet in his leg. You all right?"

"Nicked my arm—nothing serious," Tom replied, brushing at the sweat misting his eyes. The strong, acrid smell of burned gunpowder still hovered about the rocks along with the odor of scorched cloth as small, smoldering fires, ignited by bullets as they drove into the now-dead men, set clothing to burning.

"Let's get back to camp," Zell continued, moving toward the two men. His arm, now that the soaring excitement was over, had begun to throb. "Want to move. Durango might decide to come back—and we best not be there."

He glanced sharply at Tolan. "You make it? I'll catch up one of their horses if—"

"I'll get there," the homesteader said tightly, clutching his leg.

20

The women, trailed by George and Nace, came running forward to meet them before they had covered half the distance between the two camps.

"You've gone and got yourself shot," Lydia Tolan cried as she hurried up to Caleb.

He grinned, shook his head. "Ain't nothing bad," he said, making light of the wound. "Tom got winged, too."

Zell saw alarm fill Abby's eyes and tighten her lips when the blood on his arm caught her attention.

"Just a scratch," he said, and watched relief gentle her features.

"Thank God none of you got killed," Martha Fisk said, strain still evident on her lined face. "We heard all the shooting—and then the horses were running—"

"We drove them suckers off," Reuben said proudly. "Got five of them, too, right off the bat. Would've killed more if some dang varmint hadn't jumped out of the brush and give us away."

Abby had fallen in at Zell's side as they continued for the camp. Nace, an arm's length away, was silent, listening to the excited questions George and the two Fisk girls were firing at their fathers, and the subsequent answers.

"There's medicine at our wagon," Abby said. "If you'll come with me—"

She had voiced the invitation in Nace's presence, taking no pains to keep it from him. It was apparent to Tom that something had happened, that a change had taken place; it was as if she cared not at all if Nace knew her interests lay elsewhere.

"Obliged to you," Zell said, "but we've got to pull out, make camp somewhere else."

"What's that?" Lydia Tolan demanded instantly. "We ain't going nowhere till I get Caleb's leg doctored."

"Can do your fixing up while we're moving," Fisk said. "Tom figures we best get out of here fast, find ourselves another spot, because them outlaws might take a notion to come back—and I agree."

With Caleb Tolan, supported by his wife and son, hobbling painfully along, they finally reached the camp. Zell, nodding to Abby, turned away immediately and headed for his horse, the others all hurrying to their respective wagons.

Zell had not removed the saddle and bridle from the bay gelding, needed only to pull the cinch tight and swing into the saddle—taking a moment for a quick drink. The homesteaders, too, at his earlier suggestion, had left their teams in harness, and within only minutes the train was pulling out of the rock formation's shallow canyon and entering the desert.

"Which way?" Fisk, who was in the lead wagon at the moment, called out.

Tom, who had paused to throw more wood on the fire to give the impression of a still-occupied camp, motioned toward the west.

"Straight on! I'll be there with you in a bit."

Satisfied there was enough fuel loosely strung about

to keep the fire igniting itself and continuing for hours, Tom mounted the bay again and hurried to assume his position at the front of the wagons.

George Tolan rode up, swung in alongside. "Ma wants to know how far you're aiming to go?"

Zell, wounded arm now throbbing painfully and impatient with the discomfort, swore angrily. "Tell her it'll be till we find a decent place," he snapped.

Young Tolan glanced about. The desert all around them was a silvered plain broken only here and there by an occasional mesquite or smoke tree, grotesque saguaros, cholla cactus, or low-lying shrub.

"Sure don't see much hope of that out here. It's flat as a pancake."

"We'll be coming to a wash," Tom said. He had made a fold of his bandanna, was now holding it to the wound in his arm, which had begun to bleed again. "Seems to me like there's some buttes along here, too," he added in a more agreeable tone. "Have to look sharp—hard to spot them in the night."

"Ma was saying maybe it would've been best to stay right where we was. Could've held off them Mexicans—"

"Doubt it. Too many of them—and in the daytime that place would be like an oven with all those rocks."

"Yeh, I can see that," George said after a few moments. "I'll go tell Ma what you said."

"Oughtn't to be more'n an hour. I'm beginning to remember now where those buttes are—just a few miles on ahead."

Zell's memory served him well. A bit less than an hour later, the round, bubblelike formations he was searching for appeared off to their right, and he immediately veered the train into that direction.

Reaching the low, smooth hills, Zell took a course

that led the wagons into the heart of the formations; and there, pulled up against one that, eroded by time and weather, offered the flat-sided protection of a bluff, they made camp.

"It all right to light a fire?" Tolan's wife wanted to know shortly after they had halted. "Need hot water to clean Caleb's leg—"

"Keep it low," Tom replied. "We're pretty well hidden in here, but there's no use taking any chances."

The woman nodded and hurried off to see to her husband. Zell, again only loosening the gear on his horse, pulled off into a small flat area between two of the humps and laid his blanket roll. The earth was still pleasantly warm, he saw, attesting to the heat stored up by the mounds during the day. Like the rocky formation they had left, the buttes would be no place to remain once the sun was out and climbing into the sky.

His place in the camp selected, Tom doubled back to where the wagons had halted. A fire, kept small at his direction, had been built and was being used not only to heat water for Lydia Tolan's use but to make coffee and prepare food for the evening meal as well.

"Need to set up a watch," he said, drawing the attention of all. "George, you and Nace will have to go first. Split the time between now and midnight between you. I'll take over then."

"I can stand my share," Fisk said. "I ain't all that tired—and I ain't bunged up."

"Count me in, too," Tolan called from the back of his wagon. "I'll be fine soon as my wife gets done fussing over me."

"You'll do no such a thing," Lydia declared. "John and George can handle it the whole night, seems to me. They wasn't in on that shooting and ain't done nothing much but stand around and—"

Zell shook his head. "I'll be ready at midnight," he said, and pivoting, returned to his gear.

Halting beside his horse, picketed close by, Tom took out his bottle of liquor and had a stiff drink. He realized now that the wound in his arm had drained his strength to some extent, and he felt the whiskey would help.

Turning to his blanket roll, he untied the rawhide cord that held it together, and laid out the strip of canvas and the wool cover on the warm sand. He paused, glanced up, hearing a step behind him. It was Abby. She was carrying a small box filled with bottles of medicine, jars of salve, and rolls of bandage, all evidently prepared back in Ohio before the trek west had begun.

"I'm going to fix your arm now," she said firmly, sinking to her knees beside him. "You're not putting me off any longer. Take off your shirt."

He grinned, noting the sternness of her features. "Yes, ma am," he said in mock submission, and began to remove the garment.

"I prayed that you'd not get hurt—that you'd come back," Abby murmured, dabbing at the wound with a damp cloth to remove the crusted blood. "When I saw you—your arm hanging there stiff—bleeding—my heart almost stopped."

"Plenty of times I've been hurt worse than this—"

"Probably, but I didn't know you then. Anyway, a wound can mortify if it's not looked after. It pain much?"

"Some. Reckon I was lucky this time. Bullet missed the bone. Got hit in the leg once—busted the bone. I was a long time getting over that."

Abby, working quickly and efficiently, finished her ministrations with a neat bandage, and settling back, restored the items taken from the medicine kit to their place in the box, rose.

"Stay right where you are," she said. "I'll be back in a few minutes with some coffee."

Zell nodded and stretched out on his pallet. The wound in his arm still ached and was stinging smartly, thanks to the ointment Abby had applied liberally, but on the whole he felt good. It was the whiskey, he supposed—or had it been Abby? Watching her as she worked over him, seeing her close, smelling the tantalizing perfume of her—that was probably the best possible medicine for him, he thought, and then he glanced up.

"Here you are," Abby said. She was standing over him, holding a steaming cup in her hand and offering it to him.

Zell drew himself to a sitting position and took the cup from her. "Can you stay a bit?" he asked as she settled down beside him on the blanket.

"As long as you want."

"Coffee'll have to wait then," Tom said, and putting it aside, took her in his arms.

21

The scuff of a boot heel brought Zell awake instantly. Schooled in frontier life and its ever-present dangers, he remained visibly motionless while beneath the blanket covering him his hand sought and found the pistol always kept conveniently near.

It was not yet light and the desert lay in drab grayness, the silver of the night gone, the brightness of the day yet to come. The night had passed without incident, with Nace and then George Tolan dividing the first half of the watch while he, followed by Reuben Fisk, covered the last.

"Zell!"

The voice, harsh and shaking with anger, was that of John Nace. Tom rolled over slowly, moving the hand that gripped the pistol to the edge of the blanket where it would not be impeded should it be needed. It was no friendly call the homesteader was paying on him, he knew; Nace had something on his mind.

"Yeh?" he said, looking up at the man.

Beyond the man Zell could see the camp stirring into life. George Tolan was building a fire for the morning meal, and Fisk, still at his post on the crest of a nearby butte, was a vague silhouette against the lightening sky.

"I'm going to kill you," Nace said in a suppressed

sort of tone, coming closer. He was holding a rifle in his hands, had a thumb hooked over the hammer of the weapon, ready to draw it to full-cock position.

"No, I reckon you won't right now," Zell drawled, and brought the pistol into the open. As Nace stiffened, Tom sat up, stared at the homesteader. Then, "Talk. What's this all about?"

Nace's eyes flashed. "My wife—damn you to hell! You've turned her against me, taken her away—"

"Stick to the truth, Nace," Zell cut in sharply. "'Your neglect is what lost her."

"She's my wife just the same," the man said, his voice rising. "You've got no right carrying on with her like you are. Don't think your sneaking around fooled me. I know she was with you down there along the river—and then again last night!"

Martha Fisk, with her daughters and Lydia Tolan, had paused in their breakfast preparations at the fire and were looking on curiously. Abby was not to be seen. Likely she was still in the Nace wagon—and all right, Zell hoped as a sudden thought came to him. If Nace had used his fists, taken his anger out on her . . .

"You going to deny it?" the homesteader demanded.

"You want me to—that it?"

"Don't make one whit difference," Nace said, "and it'd be a lie if you did. My wife's already told me—confessed. You've broken up my marriage, Zell, and I'm—"

"Your marriage had gone to hell long before I came along," Tom said, coming to his feet. He saw Abby at that moment and breathed a sigh of relief at her appearance. She was unharmed, and as she moved to join the other women, she hesitated and glanced to where he and her husband were standing.

"Don't unload the blame on me or put it off on your wife," Zell continued. "You're responsible for what's happened. I'm plenty short on experience when it comes to something like a marriage, but it seems to me that when a man makes a woman his wife, she ought to come first, ahead of everything from then on."

"Just talk," Nace snapped, "and it don't change anything. You're the man who took Abby away from me, and I'm going to make you pay! You—you'll never have her—not if—"

Zell smiled coolly, nodded at the rifle Nace was holding. "Don't be a damn fool. I'd kill you before you could cock that gun and pull the trigger."

John Nace removed his thumb from the knurled tip of the rifle's hammer, and lowered the weapon. "Maybe so, but you won't ever get the chance."

"What's going on here?" Caleb Tolan asked, hurrying up with the aid of an improvised cane. "There some kind of trouble?"

"I'll pick the time and the place," Nace continued, ignoring the older man. "I ain't letting nobody do what you've done to me."

"Up to you," Zell said quietly, "only you best be sure the odds are all with you."

"Can be certain of that," Nace replied, now equally calm. "I'm no fool. I know I wouldn't stand a chance against a gunfighter like you."

"Damn it," Tolan shouted. "Ain't one of you going to tell me what this's all about?"

Nace, his face bleak, wheeled and stalked off toward the horses. Zell watched him for a few moments and shrugged.

"Personal matter, Caleb," he said. "I reckon it'll straighten itself out after a while. . . . Let's get the meal over with and move out."

Abby, Zell saw when the train had gotten underway, was now riding with the Fisks, leaving John Nace alone on the seat of his wagon.

It had been a complete break between them, he guessed, and wondered just how Abby really felt about it. Would she regret the separation, now that it had come to pass? Would she, deep in her mind, blame him for his part in it—for being the instrument that forced a decision upon her and Nace?

He wasn't feeling too good about it, Tom realized. He supposed he should; he had brought happiness to Abby and now they could make plans, do as they wished, but somehow the future didn't seem all that clear cut, and as the wagons rolled steadily across the desert for the distant mountains, now a blue-gray mass becoming more distinct, he wished he could get his thoughts better organized.

Not that he was sorry for his part in the matter. Abby was not only beautiful but the most desirable woman he had ever met, and her husband had wasted his chances with her by neglect and indifference. Tom doubted the man ever cared about her as a wife at all, and his attitude now of outraged husband was one of injured pride and the loss of face at having his wife turn to another man.

Zell wondered then what other members of the party thought. Back in Ohio they had been neighbors and more or less close friends. Doubtless they were aware of the situation existing between Abby and John Nace. Would their sympathies and understanding be with her, or would they side with Nace, adhering to the old standard that a woman should be a good and faithful wife regardless of all else?

He got no insight into how they felt when, at midday, they halted by a lone paloverde tree to have lunch and to rest the horses. There was nothing said, and he detected little change in their attitudes toward him. He ascribed that to the terrible, driving heat; but they had made their judgments and formed their opinions, he was certain, and such would eventually make itself known.

The brief meal over, Tom crossed openly to where Abby was in conversation with the Fisks. She greeted him with a smile.

"How is your arm?" she asked.

Zell nodded to the others present, said, "Doing fine—thanks to you."

"Expect I'd better have a look at it anyway," Abby continued, and rolling up the sleeve of the clean shirt he'd donned that morning, drew aside the bandage and made her examination of the wound.

"Seems to be healing," she reported, restoring the medicated cloth to its original place. "I'll change the dressing tonight—just be careful."

"Can bet on that—it's plenty sore," Tom said, his pulse quickening as Abby smiled at him. Turning then to Reuben Fisk, he said, "Any problems?"

"Nope," the homesteader answered. "Just that I'll be mighty glad when we're off this blasted desert. Heat's something fierce!"

"Will we be out of it soon?" Purity asked.

It was the first time the girl had spoken to him since the conversation when she'd let it be known that George had taken credit for shooting her outlaw captor. There was a sort of admiration in her dark eyes, as if she were thrilled by the love triangle that had developed and that he was part of.

"Be a few more days," he replied, and moved on to where the Tolans had pulled up. He asked the same question of them, further inquired as to Caleb's injured leg, and found all was as well as could be expected—except where George was concerned.

The younger Tolan had taken no hand in the exchange. He had nothing to say and remained somewhat apart from his parents while Zell was there. The boy, Tom recalled, noting the fact, had kept his distance all that morning, preferring to ride alongside John Nace's wagon.

George's feeling about Abby and him was plain; Nace had been wronged insofar as he was concerned, Zell realized as he turned and headed back to where he'd left his horse. To one as young as George Tolan all things were either black or white; there was never any in-between shading.

They pulled out shortly after that, still heading direct for the hills, which, after so long a time, had lost their blurred, blue-gray image and were taking on definite shape and substance. They would not reach them by dark, but they would be fairly near.

That's when he could expect John Nace to attempt something, Zell supposed—when they halted at the end of the day to make camp. Well, he'd be ready. He disliked the thought of having to protect himself from the man, hoped that it would be possible to avoid killing him, but if such came to pass, he would not hesitate: he would have no choice. He could only trust that Abby, and to a lesser degree of importance, the other members of the train, would understand.

22

The evening was quiet and tense. Nace kept to his wagon, preparing his own meal, while Abby continued her association with the Fisks. Zell, having slung his gear as usual at the edge of the camp, made no attempt to thrust his presence on any of the parties, leaving it entirely up to them to come to him if there was a need.

After the food was prepared, Abby brought him a well-filled plate along with a cup of real coffee, and sat down beside him while he ate.

"We've stirred up quite a mess, haven't we?" she said after a time.

Tom shrugged. "It bothering you much?"

Abby let her hands fall into her lap. She appeared tired, Zell thought, and her voice dragged.

"No, not too much. What will we do when we get to the Colorado? Do you still plan to leave us there?"

"It will be up to you, Abby," he replied, facing her squarely. "You can go on with the train—to California—or we can head out on our own."

"Where would we go? It's not like you had a farm or a ranch somewhere—or even a steady job—"

Tom continued to study her, a frown now pulling at his brow. "That bother you?"

Abby brushed at a wisp of dark hair straying down over her forehead, and stirred uncomfortably. "Oh, I don't know, but its all new to me—your kind of life, I mean. I've always had something to hang on to, something solid and permanent, but you—"

Zell set his plate aside and reached for his bottle of whiskey. "Can see you've been listening to the old women."

"Yes, I have," Abby said firmly, "and a lot of what they said made sense."

"That I was a no-account and not good for you, I expect," Tom said, taking a swallow of the liquor. "And they probably told you that I couldn't give you the kind of life you should have."

Abby nodded woodenly. Zell put away the liquor and drew one of the slender cigars from the leather case he carried. Biting off one end in the usual ritual, he struck a match to the tip and puffed it into life as he glanced up at the sky. The stars and moon were out, and the desert—all harsh browns, faded greens, and dull grays in the day's castigating sunlight—had changed to a broad plain of soft silver.

"Probably the truth," Zell said finally. "There's a big difference in the way you live and the kind of life I lead."

"That's what I'm afraid of, Tom. I'm not sure I could ever get used to the change."

"Be my job to make you happy—and I promise you this, you'll never go hungry or be afraid and"—he paused, having difficulty expressing himself—"and I'll always love you."

"I love you, too, Tom, but I'm not sure love will be enough. Could you give up your kind of life—so free and unattached to anybody and anything, with no responsibilities—and settle down to, well, farming? We could go on to California, you know—with the others."

Evidently Abby was unaware of the threat John Nace had made, else she would not have voiced the suggestion. It was pointless, anyway; he knew he could never be a farmer. He had changed considerably, he'd come to realize—but not to that extent.

"Have to find myself a job, hire on as a lawman somewhere, or go back to Wickenburg and ride shotgun regular on the bullion wagons for the mining companies. Good pay."

"And dangerous—"

"Maybe, but so's farming. Plenty of ways for a man to get himself hurt, and losing his shirt comes easy, too. You all being here proves that. Anyway, I'm not cut out to walk behind a plow."

"You won't even consider going on to California?"

"No, Abby, much as you've come to mean to me, I couldn't do it. First off, it would put too much strain on everybody having me around, but mainly, like I've said, being a sodbuster's not my idea of living."

"Sodbuster," Abby echoed the word, and sighed. "No, it wouldn't be," she said, and taking up the near-empty plate and coffeecup, got to her feet.

Tom followed, and for a time they stood looking out across the desert, saying nothing. Somewhere close by in the broom and weeds growing along the edges of the wash near which they'd halted, an insect began to click loudly—a lonely sound in the warm hush.

"We've settled nothing," Abby said, "nothing, except that you can't—or won't—see things my way. Maybe I'm selfish, but, Tom, I need security—something that I can tie down to. I—I can't be a drifter."

"Sounds like Martha Fisk and Lydia Tolan again," he said, shrugging. "What they never got around to telling you is that when the right woman comes along even a drifter can do some changing. Maybe he won't switch to her kind of life, but he'll make a good home for her. Might tell that to them the next time they get to handing out advice."

Abby turned to Zell. "Please don't hold it against them, Tom. They're only trying to help. They know how it has been with John and me, and they don't want me to make a mistake again."

"It could be a mistake to listen to them. They don't know a thing about this part of the country and how folks live—or what it takes. They're giving you their little one-sided farm-wife view and basing their opinions on what they've heard about a man like me."

"It's true, isn't it—the things we've been told about you? The women, the shootings, the fact that you've never held a job for long but would rather hang around a saloon drinking and gambling and dancing with those women—"

Zell removed the cigar from his mouth and glanced at its tip. The coal had died, and striking a match, he lit it again.

"Seems you've heard it all—"

"Then you can't blame them for worrying—and for trying to warn me."

"No, reckon not, but I can fault them for not telling you that a man can change if he has good reason."

"Perhaps they're not sure of that—of you," Abby said.

Zell faced her squarely. "How about you?"

"I—I'm not sure," she replied, and turned to leave. "I'll come back in a few minutes and see to your arm."

"No need," Tom said. "It's all right."

Abby gave him a long, searching look, and then continued on for the center of the camp where the others had gathered around the low camp fire to drink their coffee and hash over the incidents of the day.

Only it was not as it had been, Zell saw. Dropping to his haunches, the cigar clamped between his teeth, he let his gaze remain on the homesteaders. The easy friendliness was gone; a restraint had fallen upon the members of the train, and conversations now were brief and to the point, and there was but little laughter—none of which he knew he was welcome to participate in.

Tom shrugged at that thought, wincing slightly as pain shot through his arm. He'd gotten along fine before he met the Ohio pilgrims and he'd certainly do all right after they were gone. He didn't need them—never had and never would.

Except Abby Nace. That was a different matter for sure, and one that for the first time in his life he found himself at a loss to cope with. He'd not lie, swear to her that he'd change, be all she wished—but, on the other hand, he could not bear to lose her. But better that, he felt, than let her in for a life of unhappiness. He'd not force her to his way; it would have to be of her own free will and arrived at with no further inducement from him. He would make that clear to her—now.

Rising, Zell crossed to the camp, and nodding coolly to Fisk and Tolan and their wives, halted at the bench where Abby, Purity, and Patience were cleaning and drying the supper dishes and utensils.

"Like to say one thing to you, Abby," he began, glancing first at the two girls. "We'll be reaching the

Colorado in a couple of days. That'll give you time to think this thing through and decide what's ahead for us."

And then touching the brim of his hat with a forefinger, he wheeled, and cigar again stuck in the corner of his mouth, returned to his gear. Taking up his rifle, he continued on to the mound below the camp that he'd selected as the night's sentry post.

The camp was up well before first light as usual, making preparations to pull out. It was always good to get in several hours' travel before the day's lashing heat set in, and for that reason Zell never experienced any problems in getting the train underway.

He had saddled his horse, had his drink, and was rolling his blanket when Abby approached, bringing him his breakfast.

"Martha was going to come, show you there is no bad feeling, but I persuaded her to let me do it."

Tom took the plate and cup from Abby's hands, and hunkered on his heels. "Was nice of her—and you."

"I wanted to tell you that what you said to me last night will be fine with me. I'll make up my mind—know what I want to do by the time we reach the Colorado River."

"Good. Meantime—"

"I love you, Tom, so nothing's changed."

He smiled, put down the plate, and oblivious of anyone in the camp watching, reached out and took the woman by the shoulders. Drawing her close, he kissed her on the lips.

"Was what I was hoping to hear," he said, settling back. Picking up the plate and cup, he handed them to her. "Now, it's time we got to rolling. I'll see you at noon."

A half-hour later, with the sun still below the eastern horizon, the train moved out. Tom assumed his usual position in front and to one side—alone. George Tolan, who had studiously avoided him, had elected this day to ride with John Nace, who was bringing up the rear. The boy was not forgiving him for the wrong he believed had been dealt Nace, and Zell was too indifferent to attempt an explanation.

The Tolans were in the lead wagon, which placed the Fisk family, with whom Abby was traveling since separating from Nace, in the center. Tom glanced at her when he rode in close to tell Reuben that within the hour they would reach the mountains and be climbing a fairly steep grade to the pass in the crest and that it would be wise to save the team until then.

Fisk signified his understanding as Abby smiled and waved, and Zell had then pulled away to repeat the information to Nace, who accepted it without comment. Cutting back to the front of the train, Tom delivered the suggestion for the third time to the Tolans, who also received his words still-faced and exhibited no reaction.

The lack of response brought a wry grin to Tom Zell's lips as he returned to his customary place. He wouldn't have to put up with such for much longer—two more days, perhaps a bit less. And he'd be glad when it was over, not only because matters between him and Abby would be settled, but ...

Movement well off to the east caught Zell's attention. Jerking the bay to a halt, he narrowed his eyes to reduce the glare and studied the distraction.

Riders. About a dozen of them—possibly more.

They were coming up fast and in the lead was a man on a tall, black horse. Durango! Zell swore deeply. The outlaw had gathered more men and was returning.

23

Zell threw his attention to the mountain. It was still a mile in the distance, but there was a good chance the wagons could make it to the foot of its slope and start the ascent before the outlaws intercepted them, if they speeded up.

Wheeling his horse about, Tom rushed back to the Tolan wagon. Pulling the bay to a sliding stop, he pointed to the oncoming renegades.

"Durango—coming back! Whip up your team, you got to make it to the mountain before they cut you off!"

Caleb Tolan's face tightened. Nodding, he picked up the whip lying at his feet and lashed his mules into a hard run.

Zell waved to Reuben Fisk and John Nace. "Outlaws," he yelled, again pointing. "Follow Tolan!"

Fisk and Nace broke their teams into a gallop and shortly all three wagons were lumbering across the flat land, creaking and popping as they gathered speed, and stirring up thick clouds of dust.

Tom moved out ahead to where he could keep a close watch on Durango and his men. They had noted the increase in the train's speed, emphasized by the billowing tan clouds, and were now also moving at a faster pace.

Zell reached the foot of the mountain and drew up. It was going to be close, but with luck the wagons would make it. Then, once on the slope and climbing to the pass, the advantage would shift. It would be no chore at all for a man to take shelter behind one of the many large boulders midway up the grade, and from that position of dominance, turn back any who tried to follow—at least for a while.

Tom put his attention on the outlaws again. They were now close enough to become distinct. Joe Durango was in the lead—a half a dozen yards in front of the others. There were a number of Mexicans and several Indians—fourteen in all. Zell brushed at dry lips. Durango had come well prepared. He'd not be easy to turn back this time.

Reaching into his saddlebags, Zell dug out his bottle and had a satisfying drink. The whiskey was about gone, he noted; he'd need to replenish his supply once he got to a place where there was a saloon. Restoring the liquor to its place, he swung his eyes to the approaching train.

The Tolan wagon was racing up, careening from side to side despite its load, while the frightened mules trailing behind were frantically trying to break free. Zell watched narrowly, hoping the vehicle would not jackknife and turn over. Drawing a cigar from the case, he lit it and waited. Abruptly Tolan was there.

"Keep going! When you get to the pass, go on through, don't stop!"

Features taut, Caleb nodded, and laying the whip to his team, began to climb. Fisk arrived only minutes later. Zell shouted like instructions to Reuben, and as the wagon whirled by, Tom had a brief glimpse of Abby.

She was at the rear of the vehicle, one hand holding

on to the top bow, the other gripping something in the bed of the wagon to keep from being thrown out. She dared not wave when she saw Zell, but raised her head and smiled. In response he lifted his hand and then came back around.

Nace's wagon, whipping back and forth, had overturned. Zell saw the homesteader and George Tolan, who was beside him, sail off the seat and strike the ground with sickening force. The team, their harness torn loose, were veering off to one side and coming to a stop where they were joined by Tolan's horse, which had been tied to the rear of the vehicle.

Zell flung a worried glance at Durango and his men—now dangerously close—and raked his horse with spurs. The bay leaped into motion and in a quick rush was at the side of Nace, lying crumpled on the sand. Nearby George Tolan, conscious but dazed, was getting unsteadily to his feet.

"Grab the horses," Tom shouted urgently to the younger man. "Climb on one—bring the other one over here!"

Tolan hesitated, seemed not to understand. Zell shouted his instructions a second time as he bent over Nace and lifted him from the sand. His words registered on being repeated, and hurrying to where the pair of Morgans stood, George vaulted onto the near animal, and drumming on its ribs with his heels, doubled back to where Tom waited.

As Tolan came abreast, Zell hung Nace over the back of the off horse, secured the homesteader by wedging his hands inside the harness.

"Get out of here," he shouted to Tolan as he spun to mount his own horse. Hitting the saddle, he glanced up the slope. The first Wagon—Tolan's—was moving through the gap in the summit of the mountain, the second was close behind. He came about then as the rattle of gunshots came to him; the outlaws were now close enough to open fire.

"When you get through the pass, keep going," he yelled at Tolan, astride one of Nace's horses and leading the other at his side, swung by.

George, white-faced and leaning well forward over the Morgan's muscular neck, frowned. "What about you?"

Zell flinshed as a bullet struck the horn of his saddle and screamed off into space. "Aim to keep them off the mountain long as I can!"

Holding a tight rein on the nervous bay, he delayed until the Morgans had reached the foot of the slope and begun the climb. Strong and encumbered only by dangling harness straps and the weights of the still-unconscious Nace and young Tolan, the husky animals covered the ground rapidly, and by the time Zell had gained the bottom of the grade and swung onto it, they were already a quarter of the way up.

Durango and his men were now only yards away and firing steadily. Bullets were striking the rocks around Tom, glancing off shrilly or digging into the sunbaked soil. He as yet hadn't brought his own gun into play, intending to wait until the pilgrims were through the pass and on the opposite side of the mountain.

But Nace's accident had upset his timing. The outlaws were able to close the gap separating them from the slope much sooner than anticipated; now he would be unable to halt, make his stand at a point designed to prevent their even starting up the grade, and instead must choose a spot nearer to the summit and thereby allow Durango and his renegades a foothold.

Tom felt the shock of a bullet driving into his leg and clutched at the horn to steady himself. A sudden rage swept him. Mouthing a curse, he swung the bay in next to a clump of brush and halted. Seizing his rifle, he yanked it from the boot, and throwing himself from the saddle, crawled in behind a nearby rock—grimly ignoring the surging pain in his leg as well as that in his now-aroused arm. Settling himself, he pulled off his neckerchief, crammed it into the bleeding wound in his leg, and began an answering fire.

One of the Apaches was coming directly up the center of the trail. Hunched forward, rifle in hand, he was approaching at a trot. Tom's first bullet sent him sprawling into the dust. He saw others then, below and to either side of the path, and with bullets now splatting dully into the boulder back of which he'd taken shelter and snapping viciously about him, he began to methodically pick them off.

A lead slug struck close by his head as he leaned over to shoot, sent a shower of stinging fragments into the side of his face and neck. He brushed impatiently at the blood that began to trickle down his jaw and continued his deadly marksmanship.

The rifle clicked as the magazine emptied. Laying it aside, Zell drew his pistol and began to use it. Dust and smoke now hung over the slope in a pungent cloud and it was difficult to see the men dodging about in the echo-filled haze. Drawing himself partly erect for a better view, Zell recoiled as a bullet drove into his chest.

Through the sudden gust of pain he saw Joe Durango—hat off and hanging from his neck by the chin strap, dark skin glistening in the hot sunlight—appear a few yards down the trail.

It had been the half-breed *jefe*'s bullet he'd taken, and the outlaw was now looking to see what effect it was having. Zell leveled quick, centering on the man's head, and pressed off a shot. Durango's bearded face disappeared into a mass of blood, and lurching to one side, the outlaw leader began to tumble down the slope.

There was an abrupt lull in the shooting from below. Zell, feeling strangely light-headed, rodded the empties from the cylinder of his pistol and reloaded. Then, dragging himself to the far side of the boulder, he peered around its rough end. The outlaws were falling back. A hard grin on his face, Tom dropped two of them in rapid succession.

Others paused in their flight, hastily ducked in behind whatever bit of cover was handy, and began to shoot back. Zell emptied his weapon—wishing he had cartridges for the longer-ranged rifle—reloaded, and resumed firing.

The outlaws once again had begun a retreat, slipping, sliding, running, and falling in their haste to reach the horses they'd left at the foot of the grade. Tom drove bullets into two more of them before they were able to reach their mounts, leap onto the saddle, and race off. At that point he sank back against the rock, suddenly very weary.

But he reckoned Abby and the rest of the Ohio pilgrims would be safe now and well on their way. There was nobody in sight in the pass at the top of the mountain, and by that he guessed they had obeyed his instructions to keep moving.

A slight haze had begun to cloud his eyes, and impatient, he brushed at them, but the film did not leave. Turning, he looked for his horse. The bay was a dozen yards away, had evidently escaped the outlaws' bullets. A drink was what he needed. He'd have to get the bottle in his saddlebags, and while he was there, he'd best get a bit of rag to stuff into the wound in his chest and slow down the bleeding some. Mustering his strength, Zell tried to rise and cross to his horse, but it wasn't in him, and after two or three futile efforts he gave it up and settled back.

But he did have a cigar left in his case, and taking it out, went through the usual procedure of lighting it. When that was done, he placed his shoulders flat against the rock, and exhaling a cloud of smoke, looked out over the desert. It was going to be another hot day, he thought.

24

"There ain't been no shooting for quite a spell," Fisk said.

Contrary to Zell's instructions, the party had halted at the foot of the mountain once they were through the pass, and were awaiting him.

Abby was standing beside the homesteader looking to the top of the slope as if expecting Tom to appear at any moment. Others of the train, with the exception of Caleb Tolan, who was having considerable pain from the wound in his leg and had remained on the seat of his wagon, were nearby. Abruptly Abby turned to Reuben.

"I've got to know! Tom could be up there needing help. George," she added, facing the younger Tolan, "can I use your horse?"

"Sure you can," Caleb replied before his son could answer. "Would go see about him myself, was I able. I figure we owe him that much."

Fisk nodded. "For a man that folks said was a no-good hell raiser who never done nothing for nobody but hisself, I think he done right proud by us. . . . I'll go with you, Abby."

"So will I," John Nace said quietly. "Reuben, we can ride my team. Want to see if there's anything left of the wagon—and there's some stuff that I'm sure Abby would like to save."

Fisk said, "Good enough," in a crisp sort of way turned to George Tolan. "You look after your pa and the womenfolk while we're gone. If you need help, fire two quick shots."

The younger man nodded, and leading his horse up to Abby, helped her onto the saddle. A few steps away Nace, having gathered in the trailing harness of his team and folded the straps back to where they would no longer drag, had swung onto the back of one horse, and rifle now in hand, was waiting for Fisk to mount the other.

"Not yet," he called gently to Abby as she started up the slope. "Best you let Reuben and me go ahead. Some of that outlaw bunch could still be hanging around."

Abby, her face a mask of worry, settled back and watched while Fisk climbed onto the horse he was to ride. With no saddle and stirrups, the older man had a few moments' difficulty getting settled, but finally it was done.

"You got your gun?" he asked, glancing at Nace as he laid his own weapon across his lap.

The tall homesteader nodded. He had said very little to anyone since the break between Abby and him had occurred, was even more silent after the outlaw attack earlier that day when he had been knocked unconscious during the accident to his wagon. He seemed now to have become more thoughtful, as if struggling to understand his enemy, Tom Zell, and why the man would not only risk his own life to save him, but also would elect to remain and make a stand, singlehandedly, against overwhelming odds that he and other members of the wagon train might reach safety.

"Reckon we're ready then," Fisk said, and drummed on the ribs of his horse.

The team moved off up the slope with Abby following behind. She, too, had spoken but little since the encounter with Durango and his renegades, and now as they started for the pass, a slash in the crest well above them, a tautness, a mixture of hope and dread came over her features. But she uttered no comment and held tight to her emotions.

As they drew near the summit, Nace half-turned and glanced at her. "Stay back while Reuben and I have a look."

She nodded slowly and drew her horse to a halt. Fisk and Nace dropped from the backs of the Morgans, and bent low, rifles in hand, made their way to the pass and through to the opposite side. For a time they remained there, crouched in the blistering sunlight while they studied the opposite slope, and then satisfied there was no danger, came about and returned to where Abby waited.

Fisk shook his head when he saw the hopeful light in her eyes.

"Just can't say. Ain't nobody living in sight. Can see dead men—outlaws—everywhere."

Abby delayed for no further information, but hurried on ahead, crossed through the pass, and started down the slope. Almost immediately she saw Zell's bay gelding off to the side in the brush, and veering toward the animal, came to a sudden stop. Slumped against a large rock close by was Tom Zell.

A cry escaped Abby's lips as she slipped from the saddle, ran to where the man lay, and dropped to her knees beside him. Behind her, Fisk and John Nace, dismounting quickly, hastened to join her.

"Dead," Reuben Fisk murmured, making his examination as he knelt close by. Rising, he took the woman by the shoulders and brought her to her feet. "Ain't nothing we can do for him, 'cept bury him."

"I'm sorry, Abby," Nace said in a low voice, and turned his attention to his wrecked wagon at the foot of the grade. "Spade and shovel down there in the stuff I brought. I'll get them."

Fisk only nodded as Nace moved off, while Abby, turned from him, continued her sobbing. Then, when she had spent herself and quieted, the homesteader took her in a fatherly embrace.

"Now, I reckon I don't know all there is about what's been going on between you and Tom Zell—and your husband—but Tom's out of it now. That leaves it like it was once—just you and John—and the way I see it, you two'd best patch things up."

Abby pulled back from Fisk and stared off down the slope to where John Nace was probing about in the confused pile of their possessions as he searched for the tools he wanted. Her eyes were red from weeping and grief dragged at her features, but she had full control of herself now.

"You just plain got to be practical about this," Fisk went on. "There ain't no place in this wild country for a woman by herself. She needs a man—has got to have one—if she aims to survive. I want you to do some thinking about that."

Reuben shifted his glance to the trail. Nace had recovered the implements he'd spoken of and was returning. Fisk wheeled then, crossed to Zell's horse, and removed the tarp and blanket from its place behind the cantle.

"You best go set over there on that rock while me and John tend to this," he said as he retraced his steps and halted beside her. "There anything of his you want?"

Abby looked down at Zell's lifeless shape. She shook her head. "What I want is gone," she replied, and moved off to do the older man's bidding.

An hour later, with both Nace and Fisk soaked to the skin with sweat, they had hollowed out a grave in the hard soil, wrapped Tom Zell in his blanket and canvas, and buried him, piling rocks upon the mound to further protect him from coyotes and other varmints. When it was all done, he beckoned to Abby, and when she had returned, the homesteader took Nace by the arm and led him aside so that she might have a few moments alone at the grave.

"Your wagon busted up bad?" he asked when they were beyond earshot.

Nace, leaning on the spade, brushed away the moisture beading his forehead. "Top's smashed, but the wheels are all right and they're what counts. I figure I can load up our stuff—whatever's worth keeping—hitch on the team, and go on with you and Caleb long as we take it slow. Bound to be a few loose spokes."

"More'n likely," Fisk agreed, and glanced to Abby now coming toward them. He gave the woman's face quick study, smiled. "John, I think your wife's got a couple of things to say to you."

Nace shook his head. "It's me that's got things to say, Reuben—and I want you to hear them."

Fisk's smile broadened. Both Abby and John had apparently come to their senses, and John, his sense of chivalry coming to the fore, was going to make it easy for his wife by speaking up first.

"Abby, I know I'm the cause of what's happened to

us and what came between us. I don't fault you none for anything you've done, and I'm thanking the man we just laid away for showing me how wrong I've been."

Abby's eyes had softened. "I—I'm the one who ..." she began, but Nace waved her to silence.

"No need to say anything," he said in a hurried voice. "What I'm asking is if you'd be willing to start over, let me try to be the kind of husband you deserve—the man you saw in Tom Zell."

Abby began to cry quietly. Nace hesitated for a moment, and then rushed on. "What's past is past; we'll not think of it again, and we can make a new life together if we try."

She nodded slowly. "Just be patient—"

He moved forward a step, took her into his arms. "That goes for me, too."

Reuben Fisk cleared his throat, bobbed approvingly. "Now, let's get down there and load up your wagon. You folks are going to need all that stuff when you get to California."

46,036

Hogan

Hogan, Ray

The Hell Raiser

DATE DUE			
Mar 28 '91			
Apr 10 '91			
May 7 '91			
Nov 12 '91			
Mar 17 '92			
Jun 13 '97			
Jul 7 '97			
Mar 10 '99			
Oct 2 0 2			
APR 0 5 2008			
FEB 1 0 2014			

B